"Listen," I said. "Someone's trying to scare you into thinking you're crazy. But you're not! I see those lights. And hear that music, too."

Wait, I could tape the music. Then Great-Grandpa would know it wasn't all in his head. But that meant leaving the safety of his bed. Move, Kimball, I ordered. I watched my feet swing off the bed, just as the dazzling light blacked out. I took a deep breath, raced out the door and across the hall to my room, snatched up my radio and a new tape, sped back to Great-Grandpa's room, jumped on his bed, and let out my breath like I had swum the distance underwater. Dash sauntered in behind me. My hands shook as I took out the family history tape that Great-Grandpa and I had been recording and slipped in the new tape.

"What are you doing?" Great-Grandpa asked dully as the room was flooded with a blaze of light. It was like being photographed under a hundred spotlights.

"I'm going to tape the music."

The music played on and then, as abruptly as they had begun, the music and the lights switched off. The only sound in the room was Dash's wheezing.

"It's o . . . o . . . over," I stuttered.

I looked at Great-Grandpa. He sat as before, one hand gripping the bedpost, the other his blanket. His vacant eyes stared. Maybe he *was* crazy. All of a sudden tears filled my eyes and trickled down my cheeks. I fell back against the headboard and sobbed and sobbed. I couldn't stop. We might be killed, and no one would know.

OTHER SLEUTH BOOKS YOU MAY ENJOY

Double Helix	Nancy Werlin
Gilda Joyce, Psychic Investigator	Jennifer Allison
Haunted	Judith St. George
Lulu Dark Can See Through Walls	Bennett Madison
The Sword that Cut the Burning Grass	Dorothy and Thomas Hoobler

JUDITH ST. GEORGE

Mystery Isle

Originally titled *The Chinese Puzzle of Shag Island*

SLEUTH
PUFFIN

With fondest memories of my grandfather,
C. Byron Perkins

PUFFIN BOOKS

Published by the Penguin Group

Penguin Young Readers Group, 345 Hudson Street, New York, New York 10014, U.S.A.

Penguin Group (Canada), 90 Eglinton Avenue East, Suite 700, Toronto, Ontario, Canada M4P 2Y3
(a division of Pearson Penguin Canada Inc.)

Penguin Books Ltd, 80 Strand, London WC2R 0RL, England

Penguin Ireland, 25 St Stephen's Green, Dublin 2, Ireland (a division of Penguin Books Ltd)

Penguin Group (Australia), 250 Camberwell Road, Camberwell, Victoria 3124, Australia
(a division of Pearson Australia Group Pty Ltd)

Penguin Books India Pvt Ltd, 11 Community Centre, Panchsheel Park, New Delhi - 110 017, India

Penguin Group (NZ), 67 Apollo Drive, Mairangi Bay, Auckland 1311, New Zealand
(a division of Pearson New Zealand Ltd)

Penguin Books (South Africa) (Pty) Ltd, 24 Sturdee Avenue, Rosebank, Johannesburg 2196, South Africa

Registered Offices: Penguin Books Ltd, 80 Strand, London WC2R 0RL, England

First published in the United States of America by G.P. Putnam's Sons, 1976
This Sleuth edition published by Puffin Books, a division of Penguin Young Readers Group, 2007

1 2 3 4 5 6 7 8 9 10

THE LIBRARY OF CONGRESS HAS CATALOGED THE G.P. PUTNAM'S SONS EDITION AS FOLLOWS:
St. George, Judith, 1931–
The Chinese Puzzle of Shag Island
[1. Mystery and detective stories. 2. Maine—Fiction.]
I. Title
PZ7.S142Ch
[Fic] 75-43900
ISBN 0-399-20491-1 (hardcover)

Puffin Books ISBN 978-0-14-240841-4

Printed in the United States of America

Contents

ONE: The Oldest and the Youngest   1

TWO: An Angry Young Man   8

THREE: The Letters   15

FOUR: On the Bridge   23

FIVE: Strange Music   30

SIX: The Hidden Boat   37

SEVEN: "The Dear Folks at Home"   44

EIGHT: A Treasury of Memories   51

NINE: A Silent Docking   58

TEN: A Command Call   65

ELEVEN: The Departure   74

TWELVE: An Emergency   81

THIRTEEN: Two Alone   88

FOURTEEN: A Ghostly Performance   96

FIFTEEN: Discovery in a Desk   103

SIXTEEN: Confiding in Roger   111

SEVENTEEN: A Welcome Visitor   119

EIGHTEEN: A Broken Connection   127

NINETEEN: The Room with a Closet   134

TWENTY: Blueprint to Danger   140

TWENTY-ONE: The Captain's Secret   147

TWENTY-TWO: Night of Terror   153

TWENTY-THREE: Dash the Hero   160

TWENTY-FOUR: The Eavesdropper   168

TWENTY-FIVE: Bert and Sophie   174

Author's Note

I was an adult before I realized how colorful my grandfather's family had been. Being a writer, I decided it was up to me to tell their story.

Growing up I was lucky. My wonderful Perkins grandparents lived nearby. And there were always summers visiting family in Kennebunkport, Maine. Tales of my grandfather's father—my great-grandfather—drifted over my head . . . a sea captain for thirty-five years . . . his wife giving birth to six children at sea . . . home only a few days a year . . . retiring to a big, old house called The Anchorage. I was far more interested in playing with my cousins in their barn than listening to my family history.

And then, with World War II and gas rationing, Maine vacations ended. But I still had sleepovers with my grandparents where poking around their musty attic was my favorite rainy-day fun. One day, I found an old grocery carton filled with yellowed letters, faded journals, thirty pages of single-spaced typing, an 1881 birth certificate stamped by the American Consul in St. Helena, and sepia photographs of women in long skirts and men in jaunty straw hats.

When I asked, my grandfather told me he'd been born at sea off the coast of South Africa and the birth certificate was his. So was the journal, written in 1899 on his voyage to China to find out if the life of a sailor was for him. (It wasn't.) The single-spaced pages were his father's autobiography penned in 1887 and typed up many years later. As a boy in 1847, he had worked in *his* grandfather's grocery store. That would be my great-great-great grandfather, born in the 1700s!

Fast-forward to when my grandfather was ninety-two and living with his daughter, my Aunt Nellie. Although I recalled most of the Perkins family stories and now owned the grocery carton of memorabilia, I wanted a permanent record. So, armed with a tape recorder, I interviewed my grandfather about his boyhood in Kennebunkport, his father's experiences at sea, and his own. The result was fifty pages of priceless family memories.

Some years later, I realized I couldn't identify anyone in the old photographs. My Aunt Nellie, at ninety-six, named them all.

My Perkins family history was complete, and *Mystery Isle* is my tribute.

ONE

The Oldest and the Youngest

"Kim, did you pack your French books?" Mom called in to me from her bedroom.

"I've been studying French all summer," I called back, slipping my iPod into my backpack. Now that I'm twelve and going into seventh grade, I've learned how to field a question without really answering it. Diversionary tactics, my friend Sarah calls it.

"Mmm," is all Mom said, so I knew she wasn't listening anyway. I could hear her check her bureau drawers. Her closet door opened and shut. Then I heard her say good-bye to her plants. She was probably giving them enough tender loving care to last the three weeks we would be gone.

Mom is an interior designer at Mr. Harvey's here in New York on East Sixty-ninth Street. Bright is what everyone calls her, and I guess that's a good description.

She has bright golden hair that swings when she walks (Honey Mist rinse) and bright blue eyes. She is tall and thin (diet and Mme. Roussarky's Fitness Center). She is not all that pretty, but she knows how to dress, not too old and not too young. Just right.

Not like me. I'm tall and thin, too, but skinny thin, so that I'm too tall for preteen and too flat for juniors. And I have kinky brown hair. Not wavy or fluffy or curly, just plain kinky. Sarah tried to straighten it for me once, but it frizzed right up again, so now I keep it really short. I have blue eyes, too, but they're nearsighted like Dad's. I've worn glasses since I was seven.

One thing I know is, I'm pretty smart. My IQ is almost 150, but I'm what's called an underachiever. That means my grades stink. Except for math. Somehow logically figuring out a problem is really my bag. And I love to read. But the rest of my subjects . . . forget it.

Ms. Williams, my science teacher at the Manhattan School, told Mom and Dad their divorce four years ago came at a critical period in my emotional growth. Mom said nonsense. Ms. Williams had probably been a psychology major in college and was a frustrated psychiatrist. Dad didn't say anything. He was in the middle of divorcing Lisa, his second wife, to marry Sharon, his third, Mom having been his first.

We locked the apartment and waited for Ken, the doorman, to get us a taxi for LaGuardia Airport. Mom and I live at a snazzy Beekman Place address. What it amounts to is four servants' rooms cut off from a bigger apartment. So the rooms are really small. But Mom has fixed it up with white walls and rugs and plants so that no one realizes how tiny it is. We don't fool Ken and the other doormen, though. They know we're in a servants' wing. They kid around a lot with me, which I like fine, but Mom says she is not treated with the proper *deference*.

We made it to LaGuardia with just enough time to check in and go through security, but not too much time left over to get bored. That's the way Mom does things.

As soon as our plane was airborne and the engines settled into a steady whine, Mom opened her laptop.

"How far do my roots go back in Maine?" I asked.

Maine, that's where we were headed.

"I've told you, Kim, way back. Kimballs settled in Maine just after the Revolution," Mom said, clicking into her e-mail.

I liked the idea of having roots. I had been born and bred in New York City, as the saying goes, and who can have decent roots in all that concrete?

"What do you think Great-Grandpa will be like?" I asked.

Mom didn't look up. "Old."

I knew that. Ninety-three, that's how old. I am the last of the Kimballs. Kimball Ames Lauder, that's me, the end of the line. I am the youngest living Kimball, and Great-Grandpa is the oldest. His name is Lester Arnold Kimball, so our initials are just reversed. He is L. A. K. and I am

K. A. L. "But I mean, what will Great-Grandpa really be like?" I persisted.

Mom glanced up from her e-mail and smiled at me. Not her client smile, which is bright, but her mother smile, which is soft. And pretty.

"You're really excited, aren't you, Kimmy?"

"Well, I've never been to Maine before, especially an island in Maine."

Mom laughed. "Your father has taken you to lots of lovely islands. Puerto Rico. St. Croix. Barbados."

"But none of those is a mysterious, windswept island with a haunted house on it like The Anchorage," I said.

"The Anchorage a haunted house? Your imagination certainly works overtime." But Mom didn't sound her usual positive self.

"You're the one who told me about the ghosts in the first place," I pointed out.

"The last time I saw The Anchorage I was only seven and my great-grandfather, your great-great-grandfather, was a very scary old man with a white beard and long white hair. He talked about the ghosts to anyone who would listen. One day he cornered me and told me all about hearing Chinese music at night and seeing Chinese junks sail up the bay. I was so terrified I had nightmares for a week."

Mom's voice trailed off, and her eyes stared into the past. "Of course I realize now he was senile. After all, he was ninety-six. He died the next year at ninety-seven."

Mom giggled. "We come from long-living stock, Kim. Your old mother may be around until she's a hundred."

But I wouldn't let her change the subject. "You never told me they were *Chinese* ghosts."

"Chinese pirates, at that," Mom said. "Your great-great-grandfather was a sea captain and spent his life at sea, mostly sailing to China and the Far East. On one voyage his ship was captured by Chinese pirates. I suppose as an old man his memories went back to those days."

Chinese pirates. I had always thought a pirate was a pirate. Somehow a Chinese pirate sounded even more sinister than a regular pirate.

"I wonder if Great-Grandpa Kimball will have a white beard and be scary like his father," I said, more to myself than to Mom.

"I hope not. Getting that great big house ready for sale will be work enough without having him scary in the bargain."

"I don't think I'd ever buy a haunted house," I decided.

The flight attendant leaned down to take our orders. That was easy. It was always the same. Black coffee for Mom and Coke for me.

When the flight attendant moved on, Mom laughed. "I must say, if there are any ghosts on Shag Island, you'd certainly be the one to see them."

That was true. Ms. Williams always talks about my overactive imagination as if it were so great. Most of the time it's a pain. Like I can never not-think. If someone asks me what I'm thinking about, I can never say "nothing" like everyone else.

Our coffee and Coke arrived. Mom and I drank in silence. I finished first.

"Tell me about when you used to go to Shag Island." I pushed the button on my seat and leaned back.

Mom sent off an e-mail and then turned back to me. "First of all, The Anchorage looms huge in my memory. It probably won't be half as big as I remember it. There wasn't any electricity on Shag Island then, so it was always sort of dark and spooky. Does that please you, Kim?"

I nodded. In my mind's eye, I pictured a house like the stone mansion in the movie *The Others*. "Tell me about the seals," I prompted.

"The seals used to wake us up in the morning, barking and calling," Mom said. "Sometimes they covered the rocks beyond the cove. I'd watch them for hours from the windows by the stair landing. My mother always teased me about how the seals and I were the only ones who could swim in that cold water. I remember how Dad used to pull me out with my teeth chattering. . . ."

Mom's voice played down and she frowned. I knew enough not to say anything. When Mom was at Cornell, she had broken her leg skiing. Her parents had flown up in a private plane to see her. Their plane hit an ice storm, and both they and the pilot had been killed. Mom was in traction and couldn't even go to their funeral. After that Mom had seen Great-Grandpa only a couple of times.

But he had always acted funny, as if it had been her fault that his only son was killed. Which is ridiculous.

But that's why Mom was so surprised when a letter arrived from Great-Grandpa asking her to come up to Maine to help him close The Anchorage and get him settled in town. Mom's thoughts must have been the same as mine.

"I guess when you're over ninety like Grandpa Kimball, it's time to heal old wounds," she said, and her voice sounded funny. Mom never cries, so I was surprised. She's not like me. When I see Rhett Butler walk out on Scarlett O'Hara in *Gone with the Wind* for the tenth time on TV, I weep buckets.

Mom patted my knee. "Anyway, we're going to have a good time, aren't we, Kim?"

I nodded without answering. Going to Maine and seeing The Anchorage couldn't help but be exciting. But I wasn't so sure about Great-Grandpa Kimball. Even if there weren't any Chinese ghosts on Shag Island, Great-Grandpa was bound to be scary. I had never met anyone who was ninety-three and couldn't even guess what such an old, old man would be like.

TWO

An Angry Young Man

Mom and I were to be met at the Portland Airport by Esther Goff, Great-Grandpa's housekeeper's sister. She was to drive us to the town of Watoset. From there we would get a boat for Shag Island. It all sounded very complicated, but it worked out fine.

When we landed in Portland, I spotted Mrs. Goff right away. She was tall and thin, with gray hair pulled back in a knot. She wore big brown oxfords and just fit my mental picture of a Maine housekeeper's elderly sister. She recognized us right away, too. I guess Mom and I fit her mental picture of a couple of New Yorkers.

We stacked our luggage except my backpack in the trunk of her old Plymouth. With Mom and Mrs. Goff in the front seat and me in the back, we headed north on the Maine Turnpike.

Mrs. Goff was a terrible driver. The Plymouth had a gearshift that seemed to baffle her totally. Right in the middle of a stretch of road, she would suddenly shift, so the car would grind and shudder. And most of the way, we straddled the middle line. Every car that passed had to honk us over.

"Darn cars in such a blasted hurry," she muttered. Only she pronounced it "don cahs."

About one o'clock we stopped for lunch. At a Howard Johnson's! I had counted on a little fishing shack with nets strung from the ceiling and lobsters swimming around in big tubs. Instead, I had fried clams that had probably been dug in Maine, shipped to Chicago, cooked, frozen, and shipped back to Maine. As soon as we ordered, Mrs. Goff started to pump Mom. "I figure it's been 'bout twenty-five years since you were in these parts, ain't it?"

"About." Mom began to fiddle with her silverware.

"So that musta been twenty years more or less since your ma and pa were killed?" Mrs. Goff pressed on.

Mom froze right up. "Mmm," she mumbled. She opened her bag, took out a cigarette, and then put it back.

"Terrible thing, that aeroplane accident. Lester never really got over losing Hugh. And with Hugh being an only child, it kinda surprised me you never come up. . . ."

Mom pushed back her chair. "Excuse me, Mrs. Goff, I'm going to the ladies' room. Do you want to come, Kim?"

When we returned, our food had arrived. Mrs. Goff must have gotten the message. No one said much for the rest of the meal.

As soon as we started out again, I fell asleep, so I don't know how long we drove. A couple of shudderings, starts, and stops woke me up. We were off the turnpike and coming into a little town. I rolled down my window as we passed a used-car lot that said Watoset Car Sales. We had arrived. This was where my roots were.

There was a narrow main street that went over a clattery bridge. We passed a few run-down stores and a white steepled church. Ancient men sat on benches outside the post office. The whole town was straight out of a Norman Rockwell poster, and right away I loved it.

The streets got narrower and more twisty and a strong, fishy smell filled the air. "The ocean, Mom, I can smell it," I shouted, and stuck my head out the car window.

"Act'lly it ain't the ocean. It's the bay," Mrs. Goff said flatly. "Bert Smith'll ride you over to Shag Island and from there you got a view of the ocean."

Bay or ocean, I didn't care. I could hardly wait to see it. As soon as Mrs. Goff parked, I jumped out and ran to the edge of the wharf. A long dock ran out over the water, its gray pilings covered with scabby barnacles. Squawking gulls soared against the clear sky. The gray-green water was dotted with white sailboats. Caribbean water is fake-looking blue, as if it were dyed. And it hardly has any smell at all. This was the way an ocean should look. And smell.

I ran out onto the dock. A few gulls, perched on the pilings like wood carvings, took off with a noisy flapping. The splintery dock was cluttered with ropes, nets, buoys, an old rowboat, a couple of smelly barrels, and dozens of lobster traps stacked against a ramshackle shed.

"Ho, there, Bert Smith. Lester's folks are here!" Mrs. Goff yelled from the street in a foghorn voice. The door of the shed opened and a man's head popped out.

"Awright, Esther, keep your shirt on," he said, pronouncing "shirt" like "shut." He was a thin white-haired man in an old Red Sox cap who looked as if he were made of bones and leather. "They set to head for The Anchorage?" he called back, just as if I weren't standing right next to him.

"Ayuh, come get their luggage," Mrs. Goff shouted.

As Bert Smith started slowly past me, I guessed nothing much ever hurried him. He had left the shed door half open. Maybe there was a big tank inside where they kept all their lobsters. I pushed the door open and stepped in. As soon as my eyes adjusted to the light, I realized a man was standing by the window. I jumped.

"I—I—didn't know anyone was in here," I stuttered.

"Wal, I am," the man said.

I could see by the light from the dirty window that he was young. When he turned around, I noticed his blond hair was tied in a ponytail. He wore patched jeans and an alligator shirt.

"Bert didn't tell me anyone was going over to Shag Island," he growled. With his rope necklace and bare feet, he looked like Sarah's brother and his prep school friends. But he didn't sound like them at all. He sounded tough. And angry. "You ain't gonna be there long?" he asked. The question sounded as if he wanted the answer to be no.

What was long? I wasn't sure. "Just three weeks."

"Three weeks?" Now he really was angry. "What for? There's nothing out there but rocks and water."

I backed off a couple of feet, not wanting to answer.

"Kim," I heard Mom calling. "We're ready to go."

Glad to have an excuse, I headed for the door. "Goodbye," I murmured, and hurried out.

Bert Smith and Mom were waiting on the dock. As we started down a metal ramp toward Bert's boat, I glanced back at the shed. I couldn't see the boy inside, but I was sure he was watching us out the window. I followed Mom aboard the *Lucky Sue*. She was a white boat with a high front window and benches along either side.

"Where is that Roger?" Bert grumbled. "Always off when I need him."

Maybe Roger was the boy in the shed. I hoped not.

"Hey, Bert." There was a shout from behind us, up on the street. A boy carrying a carton of groceries ran the length of the dock, then down the ramp. It wasn't the boy in the shed at all. This boy was younger, maybe fourteen or fifteen, and not much taller than me. Sarah would probably call him cute, and in a freckly kind of way, he was. A sunburn shone through his freckles. He probably never got a decent tan. Like me.

"This here is Roger Coombs, Mrs. Lauder and her daughter." Bert Smith introduced us by waving first at Roger and then at Mom and me.

With a half nod in our direction, Roger put his carton

of groceries in the boat, then untied some ropes and jumped aboard. Bert started up the motor, and we swung away from the dock in a roar of fumes. We were off.

As we headed out to sea, we passed lots of small islands. Some were all rock. Some were all grass and trees. And some were a combination. We saw seabirds everywhere. Huge white and brown gulls glided above us or posed like statues on the rocks. Smaller, pointy-looking birds that Mom called terns skimmed and darted like acrobats. Black birds with S-shaped necks drifted in the water, then suddenly disappeared for long seconds under the surface. Then, ahead of the *Lucky Sue*, I saw round heads bobbing in the water.

"Seals!" I raced to the side of the boat and leaned out to see better.

Roger walked over to where I stood. "Those aren't seals. They're buoys for lobster traps." He laughed.

I cleaned the spray off my glasses. Sure enough, the seals weren't moving. And as we drew nearer, I could see they were different colors. I blushed and went back to my seat next to Mom feeling like a dumbbell.

Though we had been under way only forty minutes by Mom's watch, it seemed as if we had been bouncing in the *Lucky Sue* forever. The water got choppier. The sky clouded over, and a sharp wind blew across the bay. My stomach felt woozy, and my head ached.

"There's Lester's place." Bert pointed to an island straight ahead.

Shag Island! I forgot all about being seasick. Shag Island was bigger than the other islands we had passed. Even so, it didn't look very big plunked in the middle of so much water. It was bordered by great slabs of rock with dark trees filling its center. The island looked like a display out of a Tiffany window. It was a necklace of stone set in green velvet. The land rose high in the water, much higher than the other islands we had seen. And wilder.

I had been right. Shag Island wasn't like St. Croix or Barbados at all. Caribbean islands drifted in the water like rubber rafts in a pool. Shag Island looked as if survival itself were a struggle. It really *was* mysterious and windswept. All of a sudden I remembered Great-Great-Grandfather's Chinese pirate ghosts. It didn't take much imagination to see them lurking behind the tall spruce trees. Goose bumps chilled my arms, and I shivered.

THREE

The Letters

Bert Smith rang his bell three times and steered the *Lucky Sue* toward the island. A landing extended out from the rocks with a big, fat gull perched on the edge. As Bert cut his motor, the gull took off, squawking his annoyance.

Bert helped Mom and me out of the boat onto the dock. It wasn't so much of a dock, really, as a float, and it rocked under my feet. My stomach heaved. I swallowed fast so the Coke and fried clams would stay down.

"Sophie'll be waiting for us," Bert said. "Sophie Cluett's watched out for Lester these four years past. You might say she's like a housekeeper. Sophie's a fine woman."

He picked up our luggage and led the way up a ramp toward a long flight of rickety stairs that climbed at a steep angle, first in one direction, then in another. Mom followed Bert, followed by me, with Roger and the groceries bringing up the rear. We hadn't gone far up the zigzag steps when Mom and I stopped to catch our breath. We looked up. And there it was. The Anchorage.

The Anchorage wasn't just big. It was enormous. A long porch ran around one whole side of the house, with smaller porches and wings and ells and dormers jutting out every which way. Its gray shingles looked as weather-beaten as the rocks that surrounded the island. Most of the shutters hung at weird angles, and two chimneys tipped from the roof like crooked top hats. At least there was an antenna between the chimneys. I love old movies, and the sight of that antenna was as comforting as a security blanket.

The Anchorage must have been a shock to Mom, too. "It's even bigger than I remember," she said in a stunned voice.

"I'd allow it is big." Bert chuckled. "And it's fifty-eight long steps getting there."

With Mom's suitcase and my duffel bag, he headed up the rest of the stairs. After a minute, Mom followed. But I just stood there staring. All of a sudden the mainland seemed a long way off. I turned and looked back over the water we had just crossed. I saw ledges of rock and humps of islands and a few boats. And there was the coastline in the distance. It *was* a long way off.

Roger was right behind me. "How often does Bert Smith come out here?" I asked him.

"Every day. Bert and I make a circle of three islands

with mail and whatnot." Roger balanced the carton of groceries on one raised knee. "You from New York?"

"Uh-huh," I murmured, not really listening. I was more interested in getting a few things straight. "What if there's a fire out here? Or an accident or something?"

Roger shrugged. "It all works out. Nothing ever happens." He reached in his pocket and pulled out a package of gum. He took a stick, then offered the package to me. I shook my head. I broke my braces on gum once, and Mom had a fit. And this didn't look like any place to break braces.

"We went to New York two years ago. Pop got his wallet stolen. I don't care if I never go back," Roger went on, working the gum around in his mouth, "What'd you say your name is?"

"Kimball Lauder. Do you know my great-grandfather?"

Roger grinned. "Sure, everybody knows Lester Kimball. That's the Kimball you were named for?"

Why else would I be called Kimball? "Yeah, it's a family name." I started up the steps. Roger was chewing his gum so hard it cracked. The peppermint smell was driving me crazy.

Mom and Bert were waiting for us on the front porch. Tall weeds grew right to the edge of the house so the stone walk was almost hidden. The porch railing was rotted and broken. An old wicker chair slumped on three legs, and a hammock dangled in shreds. Mom looked really discouraged. I didn't blame her.

"I rang my bell like usual, and Sophie's expecting you," Bert said. "Why don't you just go on in?"

Mom hesitated. "Well . . ." she said just as the front door swung back. A tall, heavyset woman stepped out onto the porch and pulled the front door shut behind her. Instead of us going in the house, Sophie Cluett was coming out.

She held out her hand to Mom. "You're Margaret Lauder, aren't you? I recall you as a child. I'm Sophie Cluett, but you must call me Sophie. I'm so glad you made the flight safe and Esther got you up here in good time."

I could tell she was nervous by the way she ran her words together and talked too loud, like a substitute teacher coming into a new class. Sophie had gray hair like her sister, though it was cut short and swept behind her ears.

"This must be Kimball." Sophie turned to me with a smile like she was having her picture taken. I mean forced. "What a fine name. Why, there've been Kimballs 'round these parts since before the Cranes. Esther and me are Cranes. Cranes came here in—"

"We got to be getting back," Bert interrupted. "I'll take in the suitcases. Roger, you set the groceries in the kitchen."

Sophie stepped away from the door. But as soon as Bert and Roger were inside, she blocked the way with her broad shoulders. "The Kimballs and Cranes lived in Watoset a long time and always been real friendly." She hardly missed a beat. "Why, Lester used to work for my family's grocery store when him and his brother was youngsters. That was Warren, his older brother. . . ."

Mom looked stunned by Sophie's barrage of words. And I could see she didn't care to hear much more. She reached around Sophie for the door. "We're anxious to see my grandfather," she said firmly.

"Oh, I'm sure." But Sophie still held on to the door-knob. "Fact's the case, Margaret, Lester's been napping like he does in the afternoons." Worry lines wrinkled her forehead. "I oughtta warn you that he ain't so good when he first wakes up. He's apt to be cranky and some con-fused. Tell you what, s'pose you two step in the hall while I get Lester stirring. Then when he's set, you can see him."

The door bumped against Sophie's back. She moved aside as Bert and Roger came out.

"Regards to Lester. His mail and newspaper's on the front table." Bert patted Sophie's arm as he passed. She looked at him and gave a quick little nod. He nodded in return. It was almost like a signal, though no one seemed to notice but me.

Roger grinned. "'Bye, Kimball, see you tomorrow."

"Good-bye, Roger." I smiled back at him. With a wave, he followed Bert across the yard and down the stairs. If you liked freckles, Roger *was* cute.

"Now, let's get it over with," Sophie said as if we were all about to take an exam. She opened the door and showed Mom and me into the front hall. It smelled musty and was so dark I could hardly see.

"Wait here." Straightening her shoulders like a soldier,

Sophie slid back a set of double doors and disappeared into another room.

"Well." Mom put down her laptop and opened her bag for a cigarette. "Well," she said again as she lit it. Mom isn't speechless often.

I knew what she meant. I felt overwhelmed myself. What had we gotten into? Setting my backpack on a table, I looked around. Now that I was more used to the light, I could see we stood in a wide hall. It was loaded with furniture. Dark, heavy chairs, two long tables, a bookcase full of old books, busts, portraits, and antlers on the walls filled the room. An umbrella stand and a hat rack guarded either side of the front door. If this much stuff was crammed in the hall, what did the rest of the house look like? I couldn't imagine.

"Now what's all this about?" We heard Great-Grandpa's voice before we saw him. Then he appeared in the doorway. My first reaction was relief that he didn't have a white beard and long white hair. But he did have a bristly mustache and thick salt-and-pepper eyebrows that ran together in one scowling line. And he was old. Very old. His face and ears were so long it was as if they had stretched with age. He was bent and leaning on a cane. And he looked very angry.

Sophie came running up beside him. "But, Lester, you remember you asked Margaret to come help you get The Anchorage ready for sale." She put her hand on his arm.

He threw it off impatiently. "Sell The Anchorage?

Never. By thunder, Sophie, what's gotten into you?"

"But we talked it all out and decided it'd be best to sell this old place and settle you in town." Sophie's voice was pleading.

"You want to have me put in the poor farm, that's what. I'll never sell The Anchorage, Sophie, and you know it." Great-Grandpa tapped his cane on the floor.

He was terrifying. At least he hadn't noticed Mom and me. I hoped he never would. But Mom surprised me. She crossed the hall and put out her arms as if to hug him.

"Grandpa, it's me, Margaret Kimball Lauder, your granddaughter. And this is your great-granddaughter, Kimball. We were so happy to get your letter and know you needed us. Now we're here to help."

Mom must have taken Great-Grandpa by surprise, too. He backed away a step. "Margaret . . . Hugh's child . . . so many years . . ." he stammered. His pale-blue eyes blinked fast. Then he shook his head as if to clear it. "But what letter? I didn't write you a letter."

"Why . . . why . . . I got it over a month ago." Mom looked dumbfounded. "I wrote you right back saying we'd be glad to come."

"You remember, Lester," Sophie interrupted him. "Margaret's letter arrived the day we had that bad storm. It's on your desk." She ran into the next room and came right back with Mom's letter.

With a frown, Great-Grandpa put on a pair of black-rimmed glasses, took the letter from Sophie, and carefully read it. When he was finished, he looked right at Sophie and thumped his cane so hard I felt the floor shake. "I never saw that letter afore in my life!"

"But you did, Lester, don't you remember how pleased you were to get it?" Sophie contradicted. "We talked about how nice it would be to have family and young people in the house again."

"Don't tell me that. It's not true." Great-Grandpa sounded panicky. "I never wrote a letter to Margaret and, till now, never saw this one from her." He pulled off his glasses and shoved them back in his pocket. Then he turned on his heel and limped off through the double doors and out of sight.

Sophie tried to smile at Mom and me, but she looked close to tears. "I was afraid of that. I feel so bad. Some days he's worse than others. He's a good man. It's just that he gets impatient with himself for forgetting. . . ." Her voice petered out. She gave another quick smile of apology, then hurried after Great-Grandpa, leaving Mom and me to stare at each other in amazement.

FOUR

On the Bridge

After Sophie left, Mom and I didn't say a word. Then Mom lit a second cigarette from the butt of her first. It was a bad sign. Mom chain-smoked only when she was really uptight.

"Maybe Bert hasn't left yet," I whispered. Great-Grandpa didn't have a white beard and long white hair, but he couldn't have been any scarier.

Mom put a firm hand on my arm. "Now hold it, young lady. We're here to help, and that's what we're going to do. You have to realize how old Grandpa is. He's forgotten he wrote us, that's all."

When Mom calls me "young lady," there's no use arguing. I walked over to the bookcase and studied the shelves of ancient books. I picked up a couple of 1984 *National Geographics* and flipped through them. Mom stood staring at a portrait of an old woman as if it really interested her.

"Lester's quieted down some." It was Sophie. She was marching toward us through the double doors. "He's on the Bridge with his telescope. It always calms him down."

"I'd forgotten about the Bridge," Mom said.

"It's really just a sun porch, but Lester's pa fixed it up with all the equipment he had on the bridge of his ship," Sophie explained to me. "You know, a telescope, barometer, compass, and whatnot. It's been called the Bridge as long as I can remember."

That settled, Sophie turned to Mom. "Now let's get you two situated in your rooms. I bet you'd like to wash up, too." She reached for Mom's suitcase by the table, then stopped short. "Oh, look, Lester's mail and newspaper. I'd forgot Bert brought 'em." She picked up the mail and quickly sorted through it. Slipping two of the letters into her apron pocket, she held the rest out to me, along with the newspaper.

"Why don't you take Lester's mail and paper out to him, Kimball? He loves his paper, and he'll be real pleased. The Bridge is right through the living room." Sophie pointed to the room beyond the double doors like a Roman emperor sending a gladiator to the lines.

"Oh, I don't think I should," I said quickly.

"There's no reason not to," Mom chimed in. "And you'll win a few points with Grandpa." Mom sounded as if she were kidding, but I knew she wasn't. Her expression was strictly no-nonsense.

I took the mail and paper from Sophie and headed

through the double doors into a long, empty room. Empty of people, that is. Otherwise, full. Full of large, dark furniture, most of it covered with white sheets like so many hunchbacked ghosts. Bookcases, gloomy portraits, a lumpy-looking sofa, and more antlers cluttered the room. The curtains were closed so it was dark. And spooky.

I headed toward the fireplace at the far end of the room. Two huge, bigger-than-life statues jutted out on either side of it. When I got closer, I saw one was an old-fashioned woman in a long blue dress and one was a man in a black suit with a black top hat. They looked like giant wedding-cake figures. Were their shiny painted eyes following me? I edged around the fireplace toward the door beyond it.

With my eyes still on the statues, my foot came down on something thick and soft. And alive. *Aaaaoooo*, it howled.

Eeeeek, I screamed in turn and jumped back. The "thing" took a few steps toward me, sniffed once or twice, then turned away. With a whimper, it flopped down by the fireplace. It was just a dog. Nothing to be afraid of. But I was whimpering, too, and my heart pounded in my throat.

"Dammit, Sophie, you know Dash sleeps by that door," I heard Great-Grandpa shout from the next room. I couldn't have answered if I had wanted to. Which I didn't. Roots or no roots, what I wanted right now was out.

"Well, what is it?" Great-Grandpa yelled.

The dog's narrow face drooped over his front paws as he looked up at me. The two statues stared into space over my head. The Bridge, or whatever it was, couldn't be weirder than this room. I knocked on the door.

"Come in," boomed Great-Grandpa's Billy Goat Gruff voice.

When I opened the door, I was startled by a burst of light. The long, narrow room, more porch than room, was all enclosed by glass, and the setting sun beamed an orange glow over everything. There were a couple of wicker chairs and tables scattered around. Clocks and a compass and a barometer and official-looking equipment hung on one wall. The doorknob, the chair and table legs, and a railing around the window were all knotted with fancy ropework I knew was macramé. Mom had taken a course once to learn how to do it. Great-Grandpa sat on a stool, looking through a long brass telescope that was pointed toward an open window and the water. He didn't turn around.

"Why in thunder are you pestering poor Dash, Sophie?" he growled.

"It's me." I sounded as if my heart were still in my throat. Which it was. "I brought your mail and paper." I laid them on a chair and started to back out the door.

Great-Grandpa looked up. "So it's you, eh?" His black-and-white eyebrows scowled as he eased himself off the stool.

"I'm sorry I stepped on your dog," I apologized.

"So you think I got a letter, do you?" he asked.

"I don't know what's in the mail, sir. I didn't look at it."

"No, no, girl. I mean that letter Sophie just showed me. And what about that letter your mother claimed to have got from me?" Great-Grandpa snapped. "Did you see my letter?"

"Well . . ." I knew he wanted me to say no. But scared or not, I wasn't about to lie. "Yes, I saw your letter to Mom. You asked us to come up here."

"Was it my handwriting?"

How would I know what Great-Grandpa's handwriting looked like? "I don't know."

"Well, show it to me and I'll tell you soon enough if I wrote it or not," he ordered.

"Mom didn't bring it with her, I guess. But I remember she wrote you right back." Our conversation was beginning to sound like a routine between a couple of TV comics.

"There, that proves it. If your mother can't produce it, I never wrote it. And I never saw the letter she wrote to me till today when Sophie pulled it out of my desk like a rabbit from a hat." Great-Grandpa leaned closer. "Since I broke my ankle last winter, I can't manage those cliff stairs. I got to depend on Sophie for my mail. How'm I to know if I'm getting it all?" His breath was strong with the smell of cloves.

We were nose to nose, so to speak, and if he wanted me to agree, I was glad to oblige. Besides, I remembered Sophie taking two letters from the pile of mail. Had they been hers or Great-Grandpa's?

"I guess you're right," I said.

"'Course I'm right." He rapped his cane on the floor like a little clap of applause.

That decided, I reached back for the doorknob. But before I could turn it, Great-Grandpa's hand flew out and grabbed my shoulder. His gesture was so sudden I let out a yelp. His fingers were like a vise. Great-Grandpa was shorter than me, and thin, so I was really surprised by his strength. My knees sagged as he steered me toward the open window. I could see the tops of the trees beyond it and could guess it was a long way down.

"Look through that, girl." He tapped a leg of the telescope stand with his cane.

I went rubbery with relief and had to grip the telescope for support. It was cool and solid under my hand. With shaky fingers, I took off my glasses and looked through it with my right eye. Everything was a blur.

"Nice," I said.

"What do you see?"

I fast put my glasses back on and stood up to see what I should be looking at. But Great-Grandpa caught me.

"You need glasses? No Kimball wears glasses." He pulled his own glasses from his pocket. "I wear these just for reading. I bought 'em in the dime store years ago."

Did he think I wore glasses because I looked good in them? "My dad wears glasses." There, let the Lauders take the blame.

It seemed to satisfy him. "If you wear glasses, the telescope needs adjusting, and I don't aim to fiddle with it now." He took out a little brush, dusted the eyepiece as if I had smeared it all up, then sat down on his stool again.

"Mmmm," he murmured as if he saw something really exciting. A whale? A shipwreck? He seemed to have forgotten me.

I retreated toward the door. "Well, good-bye." Did he wonder if I meant good-bye-for-now, or good-bye-forever? He probably hoped, like I did, that it was good-byeforever.

"Wait," he grunted. Then he turned around and looked at me, really looked at me for the first time. His faded blue eyes studied my face. "You're wily and scrawny, a real Kimball," he said finally. "There's been a Kimball in this house since it was built in 1925." He called it nineteen two five. "Maybe you and The Anchorage will take a fancy to one 'nother."

Great-Grandpa's frown was as fierce as ever. But as he looked me in the eye, he winked. The wink was over so fast I wasn't sure there had been one. I gave a half wave in return and stepped back into the darkness of the living room. My thoughts were whirling as I felt along the floor with my feet for the dog. It had been a strange conversation. And an even stranger wink.

FIVE

Strange Music

By the time I reached the front hall I really had to go to the bathroom. That's the way I am. Right at the most exciting part of a movie, I have to go. But the front hall was empty. Mom and Sophie must have taken everything upstairs. I raced up the wide wood-paneled staircase. It went up half a flight to a landing, then turned, and went up another half flight. Flowered brown draperies were drawn across the width of the landing. I pulled one of them back. There was a row of four big windows. I looked out. I could see down past the trees to the water. This must be where Mom used to watch the seals. I pressed my nose against the glass and searched the water but didn't see anything that might be a seal.

I ran up the rest of the stairs. At the top I stopped short. There was nothing but a long hall of closed doors in front of me. "Mom?" I called. I felt like Alice in

Wonderland chasing the White Rabbit down the passageway of locked doors. Only I hoped these weren't locked. I knocked on the first door to my left.

Only desperation to find a bathroom gave me the courage to open the door. I peeked in. There was a huge, canopied four-poster bed in the middle of the room surrounded by dark curtains. It wouldn't have surprised me to see King Henry VIII laid out behind those curtains. It was that kind of room. I shut the door. Fast.

"Mom?" I tried the door to my right. Locked.

I went up three steps and knocked on the first door I came to. One of these rooms just had to be a bathroom. I turned the doorknob. It was some kind of playroom, with a green felt-covered pool table in the middle of it, and rows of antlers on the walls. Were there any more moose or deer left in Maine?

The next room was jammed with trunks and storm windows. This house was too much. A million rooms and not a bathroom in sight.

"Mom! Help!"

A door slammed somewhere, and I heard footsteps running.

"Kim, for heaven's sake, what's wrong?" Mom came charging down the hall. She looked worried. She grabbed me by the shoulders, gave me a quick once-over, then hugged me. It felt good to be hugged. And safe. Over Mom's shoulder I saw Sophie come panting up behind us. She looked worried, too.

"Well, what is it?" Now that Mom saw I was all right her voice was sharper.

"I was looking for a bathroom. You weren't around . . . then I got scared . . . and I have to go."

"'Course you need a bathroom, and there ain't many despite the size of this house," Sophie sympathized before Mom could say anything. "And this dark old place can be pretty frightening. Since we got our own generator for electricity, Lester and me are pretty careful with the lights."

"A bathroom, please," I gasped.

Sophie pointed to a closed door farther down the hall, and I raced for it. The bathroom had the biggest tub I ever saw on little claw feet. The toilet had a long chain to pull, and an old cracked sink was set in a wooden stand. At this point, it looked better than the ladies' room at the Waldorf Astoria.

"We'll go right down and have supper," Sophie said when I came out. She led the way to the staircase.

I tugged at Mom's sleeve and held her back. Sophie didn't seem to notice. She kept talking away.

"Can we go home in the morning? Please?" I whispered.

Mom put her arm around me. "We're both hungry and tired. In the morning I promise things will look different." I recognized the old diversionary tactics. Mom didn't say yes. Or no. She didn't even say things would look better. She just said different. That might mean worse. I sighed.

To my surprise, supper tasted really great. We ate in the kitchen, a big high-ceilinged room with a huge woodstove. Sophie had fixed supper and by the time we sat down the sun had set. Two kerosene lamps threw nice kitcheny shadows on the walls. And there were nice kitcheny smells: wood burning, biscuits in the oven, and coffee perking. I compared it to our kitchen in New York with its stainless steel appliances, and black-and-white striped wallpaper (to create height), and white curtains pulled over a nonexistent window (to create depth). It was no contest. The Anchorage kitchen was what kitchens are all about.

Great-Grandpa and Sophie had already eaten. "We're up early and have breakfast done with by six thirty," Sophie explained, pouring cream on my blueberries. "Up here we eat dinner at noon and supper at five." Sophie frowned as Mom lit a cigarette and looked around for an ashtray. When Sophie made no move to get one, Mom used her butter plate; I could see that Sophie didn't like it. "Same ways we get up early, we go to bed early, too. Why, I'd wager that Lester's in bed right now."

I looked up at the big old clock by the stove. Almost nine o'clock. I was tired but decided to make my move anyway. "Can I watch TV for a while, Mom?"

"Why, we got no television here, child," Sophie answered instead.

I felt like an idiot. "I thought I saw an antenna on the roof."

"That's for Lester's radio. It's our linkup to Bert in Watoset, and the only contact we got with the main."

It took a minute for what she said to sink in. "You mean there's no telephone either?"

"My, no. How could we run a phone line out here?" Sophie clucked at the thought. "We got no cell reception, so cell phones don't work neither and 'course we got no computer. I put my portable radio in your room, Kimball, if you want something to listen to."

"Thanks, Sophie."

I didn't need a radio. I had my iPod. But no phone? That meant Mom couldn't even get dial-up service for her laptop. I'd never been anywhere that didn't have access to a phone, and it was a funny feeling. I mulled it over as Sophie stood up and started to stack the dishes.

"Let me help, Sophie," Mom offered through a yawn.

"No, thanks. You're tired, and so am I," Sophie said. "I'll wash 'em in the morning."

Mom didn't argue. I didn't see a dishwasher, so I didn't argue either. Besides, all of a sudden I was tired, too, really tired. After Sophie finished rinsing, the three of us headed up the stairs. A light had been turned on in the hall, and its yellow glow was cheerful. Great-Grandpa must have left it on for us. Sophie led us down the hall, up three steps, to the right, then to the left. We seemed to be in some sort of wing. There was a center hall with two closed doors on each side. Beyond those were two more doors, both open. I noticed Great-Grandpa's dog Dash curled up on a little rug asleep in front of the farthest door to the left. He raised his head to look at us but didn't stir.

"That's Lester's room. And it was his father's room

before him. And this is your room, Kimball." Sophie pointed to the door opposite it, and we went in. I perked up. Instead of the dark furniture and brown flowered curtains I expected, my room was a cheerful blue. There was a rag rug on the floor and a quilt for a bedspread. Two hurricane lamps on a blue dresser turned on with a switch. My duffel bag was on my bed.

"Where's your room, Mom?" I asked.

"Just down the hall and around the corner," Sophie answered for her. "You and your great-grandfather have this wing all to yourselves. And you even have your own bathroom." I knew in The Anchorage a bathroom was real VIP treatment, and I was grateful.

Mom squeezed my shoulder and kissed me. "I'm absolutely dead, baby. Sleep tight, and I'll see you in the morning."

She and Sophie were hardly out of the room before I slipped out of my flip-flops and climbed into bed in my T-shirt and pants. I didn't unpack, wash my face, brush my teeth, put on elastics for my braces, open a window, or close my door. I didn't even brush out my hair, which meant it would be a snarly mess in the morning.

I weigh only a hundred pounds, but the bed sagged under me as if I weighed two hundred. It had to be the softest mattress I ever lay on. Mine at home was like a board so my posture would turn out terrific. But this one folded up around me like a goose-down sleeping bag. I must have fallen asleep right away.

◆ ◆ ◆

Chinkley-chime-chime. My eyes flew open.

Chinkley-chime-chime. I lay still as a mouse trying to get myself together. I couldn't even place where I was. All I knew was my heart was pounding, and I was hot. Very hot. The air conditioning must have gone off.

But I wasn't in the apartment. I was in Maine. In Great-Grandpa's house. I had too many blankets on, and the windows were closed. I always dream when I'm too hot. I threw back the quilt, the funny tinkly music still clear in my head.

For a long time I lay on the unfamiliar bed, with the house inky black around me. In the very back of my mind, without even putting the idea into a real thought, I knew I was waiting for more of that tinkly music. The house creaked and groaned. From beyond my closed windows I heard the muffled gong of a bell buoy and the wind rustling through the pine trees. But there was no more music. As I began to sink into a fuzziness that's not sleep or waking, but a foggy state in between, a memory lapped over me. The music had been strange and yet familiar. I had heard it before, eating out with Mom. A restaurant . . . the House of Fong . . . Chinese music . . .

SIX

The Hidden Boat

On vacation I usually sleep late, so I was surprised to see how dark it was when I woke up. I raised my head to look out the window. Nothing. It wasn't dark, and it wasn't light. Fog, that's what it was. I shivered and snuggled deeper under the covers.

But there was too much noise from across the hall to sleep. A window slammed. A drawer squeaked open, then banged shut. Great-Grandpa cleared his throat and coughed. He blew his nose and coughed some more. Then his footsteps, with the extra tap of his cane, went down the hall. The click-click of Dash's nails followed him. I punched my pillow and turned over to go back to sleep.

The music! My eyes flew open as I remembered the funny Chinese music. What a crazy dream. Still, it had seemed so real. Maybe one of those Philippine wind chimes had been chiming. But with the windows shut, what would have set it off? By now I was wide awake. I might as well get up and take a look around. I rolled out of bed and checked the whole room. There was nothing to hear but the sound of the gulls and nothing to see but the furry fog trying to get in. Mom's talk yesterday about Chinese pirates and Chinese ghosts must have got me dreaming, though my dreams usually make some sort of sense. . . .

All of a sudden my old-fashioned blue room didn't seem as cozy as it had the night before. I opened my duffel bag, put on a clean T-shirt, pants, and my sneakers, brushed out my snarly hair the best I could, raced in and out of the bathroom, and made a beeline for the hall. As I headed for the stairs, I wondered which room in the Alice in Wonderland maze of doorways and halls was Mom's. And if she was up yet. I doubted it.

The kitchen was easy to find. I followed the smells. Great-Grandpa was already seated at the table while Sophie worked at the sink. Dash lay by the stove. I got my first really good look at him. He was an old short-haired dog with a long curved tail. His face and throat were frosted white. When I came in, he heaved himself to his feet, walked over on stiff legs to inspect me, then tottered back to the stove.

"Well, good morning, Kimball. I didn't expect to see you down so early." Sophie smiled.

"Good morning." I'm practically never tongue-tied, but it was all I could think of to say. For something to do, I looked up at the clock. Five of six. No wonder Mom wasn't down yet.

Sophie dished me a big bowl of oatmeal. I couldn't ever remember eating oatmeal before. Usually I have juice and a bagel. Sophie dotted the oatmeal with butter, then sprinkled on brown sugar. It looked good.

Great-Grandpa didn't seem to have anything to say either. I took the chair opposite his and started on my oatmeal. I ate halfway through it before I glanced up at him. He looked terrible. His face was as gray at The Anchorage shingles, and his eyes were framed by dark circles. He stared over my shoulder as if I weren't even there, and when he picked up his coffee cup, his hand was so shaky, he spilled coffee on the tablecloth. Last night he had seemed old, but energetic. This morning he seemed just plain old.

Sophie must have noticed me gawking. She slid a cup of hot chocolate in front of me. "We got a busy day, Kimball. I hope you can help me wash windows so they sparkle. I want The Anchorage to look its best." She put her hand on the back of Great-Grandpa's chair. "Doug Tate is coming out from Watoset to get a good look at the house today, Lester. You remember."

But Great-Grandpa didn't hear her. At least he didn't answer. His eyes were still focused over my shoulder in a stare that was beginning to make me squirm.

"You remember Doug Tate, don't you, Lester?" Sophie's voice was as grating as fingernails on a blackboard. "Doug is the Realtor over in Watoset who's going to put The Anchorage on the market. Right away, while Margaret and Kimball are here to help." Sophie moved her hand to

Great-Grandpa's shoulder as she leaned over him, practically shouting in his ear. I wanted to yell at her to stop, but I just kept shoveling in the oatmeal.

"Lester, pay me mind now. Tell me you hear what I say." This time Sophie really did shout.

"Ayuh, I hear. Old Alfred Tate's nephew is coming about the house." Great-Grandpa nodded, then kept on nodding like he couldn't stop. His pale-blue eyes looked blank. Suddenly I felt sorry for him. He seemed so frail and shrunk up in his chair, gazing into space and nodding his head.

"Doug wants to get measurements and check everything out so he can give you a fair estimate." Sophie towered over our table, and I shrank up, too. The oatmeal tasted like lumpy mashed potatoes, but I kept eating away. Great-Grandpa and I were a couple of wind-up toys, him nodding and me eating.

"It's for your own good, Lester, and you know it," Sophie insisted.

Great-Grandpa reached up and touched her arm. His hand was crisscrossed with blue veins and covered with brown old-age spots. "You want me out of The Anchorage, don't you, Sophie?" His voice trembled.

Sophie shot a quick look at me. "Ah . . . ah . . . Kimball, for goodness' sakes, what do you think? With all the excitement last night, I left my sheets on the line. They'll never dry if I don't hang 'em in the cellar. Could you please get 'em in for me? The basket is in the back hall."

Even a two-year-old would know she wanted to get rid of me. And I was twelve. Still, what could I say? Reluctantly, I pushed back my chair and headed for the back hall. As I picked up the laundry basket and opened the door, the clammy air hit me like a slap with a wet washcloth. Guessing the clothesline was nearby, I started through the tall grass. Before I'd gone twenty feet, my sneakers and pants' legs were soaked.

What was going on that Great-Grandpa looked so awful this morning? Something for sure, or Sophie wouldn't have zapped me out of there like that. With my mind still back in the kitchen, I walked right into a soaking wet pillowcase and scared myself silly. I stopped and began to take down the rows of soggy sheets.

Urrgh. Urrgh. Urrgh. Seals. That barking grunt just had to be seals.

I dropped the rest of the wet sheets in the basket and ran to the edge of the drying yard. The tops of the dark spruce trees spiked through the fog like church steeples. Beyond the trees, the barking of the seals sounded close enough to be right on the rocks below. I glanced back at The Anchorage. Though I couldn't see, I was sure the stair-landing windows looked out on this same view.

There was a path on the edge of the yard that led downward, with stones wedged in for steps. I started down. I sensed, rather than saw, when I had almost reached the bottom. The trees thinned out, and low bushes, strung with cobwebs, bordered the path. Then I saw the water, flat and calm as the reservoir in Central Park. I stood for a minute listening for the seals. From the drying yard they had sounded as if they were right by the water's edge. Now I couldn't hear them at all. Only the slip-slap of water on the pebbly beach and the shrieking of the gulls broke the damp silence.

Putt-putt-putt. The chugging noise sounded like a motorboat. That must have been what scared away the seals. It was probably some fisherman out early. But instead of the noise fading away, the boat seemed to be coming closer. How could anyone see in this fog? Maybe my yellow T-shirt glowed like a lighthouse and was leading him in. Only that thought didn't seem so funny when the bow of a boat suddenly cut through the mist, just down the beach from where I stood. The motor shut off. Without even thinking, I raced back up five or six steps and ducked down behind some thick shrubbery. If it had been a sunny day, I probably wouldn't have hidden. But there was something eerie about the swirling fog and thick quiet.

A man dressed in a rain slicker and black boots climbed out of the boat and pulled it from the water. I heard the boat scrape across the rocky beach, but instead of leaving the boat just above the waterline, he hauled it all the way up to a clump of boulders not far from where I hid. Turning the boat on its side, the man worked it in between two rocks that formed a kind of slot. The boat seemed to fit right in, as if it had been stored there before.

Then the man covered the opening with branches. The hiding place was so neat no one passing by would ever have noticed it.

I watched spellbound, not trying to figure out why the man was doing all this or even who he was, Until he took off his rain slicker and turned around. He seemed to be looking right at me. I froze into instant ice. It was the young man I had talked to in the lobster shed the day before, the young man who had been so angry that Mom and I were coming to Shag Island.

SEVEN

"The Dear Folks at Home"

Even though the young man seemed to be looking at me, his expression didn't change. He stretched his arms over his head and yawned. Then he turned and started down the beach. In the opposite direction. He must not have noticed me. Long after he had disappeared into the fog, I didn't move. I heard the clang of the bell buoy and the calling of the gulls back and forth. A seal barked. Then another. At this point, I couldn't have cared less about seals.

Still bent over, I scrambled back up the slippery path as fast as my sneakers would take me. At the top, I had to stop and catch my breath. The Anchorage loomed above me like a huge ark in a sea of fog. A safe ark. I picked up the heavy laundry basket of wet sheets and staggered into the house with it. Sophie was at the sink washing dishes, but Great-Grandpa was gone.

"Sophie, there's a boy on the beach . . . he hid a motorboat in the rocks . . ." I blurted out, sliding the laundry basket across the floor.

Sophie's back was to me so I couldn't see her face. But her hands stopped washing. She didn't move or say anything. Then she turned around. "Now what's this, Kimball?" She laughed. That is, her mouth laughed, but her eyes didn't.

I took a deep breath the way we're taught to do in speech class so we won't be nervous. "Outside just now, I heard seals barking. But when I went down to the water, they were gone. What I saw, instead, was a boy bringing a motorboat up onto the beach. He hid it between some rocks. . . " My story trailed off. It didn't sound as scary in the telling as it had in the happening. For once Sophie didn't say anything. She just dried the same dish over and over.

All of a sudden I had an idea. "Maybe the boy lives here. Are there other houses on the island?"

Sophie shook her head and turned back to her dishes. "My, no, it's all Kimball property. But July and August are somethin' around here. Youngsters toot all over in their boats, water-skiing and raising cain. Prob'ly that boy don't want his folks to know he's got a boat, so he hides it here. More'n likely one of his chums drops him off so he can use it. No harm done. By September the summer people'll all be gone like the rest of the summer pests."

Sophie's explanation made sense. Sort of. But that boy didn't look like the water-skiing type. Still, I didn't want to start an argument that I was bound to lose. Sophie was so . . . so . . . somewhere in the back of my mind was the perfect word to describe her, but it wouldn't come to me. "Anyway, here are your sheets," was what I came up with.

Sophie didn't even look at them. "Now when your ma comes down we can get to work cleaning the house."

"Ma is down and ready to work." Mom stood in the doorway. She had on jeans and her blond hair was tied in a red bandanna. Even in work clothes Mom looks good.

Sophie blushed. "Oh, I didn't mean you were late getting up or anything, Margaret. It's just that—"

"A cup of hot coffee, and I'm set for the morning," Mom interrupted. I guess interrupting was her way of handling Sophie's garrulity. That was the word I wanted. It was a vocabulary word meaning talkativeness. In school we get vocabulary lists to memorize, supposedly for our own good. But if we score well on the standardized tests, the school looks good, too. Sometimes, though, like now, the words come in handy. Garrulity just fit Sophie.

She handed Mom a cup and saucer from the cupboard by the sink. Mom poured herself some coffee and sat down to drink it. I was dying to tell her about the funny Chinese music. And the boy with the boat. I knew Mom wouldn't pass it off like Sophie had. But I wanted to wait until we were alone.

"What a beautiful cup and saucer." Mom ran her fingers around the inky blue and white patterned cup. She lifted the saucer and looked at the bottom. Her eyebrows shot up. "Is there more of it?"

For an answer, Sophie opened both cupboard doors. A set of the blue and white china filled both bottom shelves. "Lester's father brought it back from Shanghai. He sailed all over the world, but this is all that was left from his travels."

Mom nodded and strolled over to the cupboard. I could tell by the supercasual way she walked how excited she was. In a junk shop, the more casual she acts, the better the find. "This looks very valuable, Sophie."

Sophie shrugged. "I reckon. Lester is fond of it, so I'm careful how I handle it." She finished the last of the dishes and slipped the dishpan under the sink. "We got a lot to do before Doug comes, dusting, vacuuming, opening the drapes, washing the windows—"

Mom cut her short. "Who's Doug?"

"Douglas Tate, the Realtor. He's coming this morning to look over The Anchorage. He may even have a buyer."

Mom looked astonished. "But last night Grandpa wouldn't even discuss selling."

"Let's say Lester's more amenable this morning," Sophie retorted.

"Amenable" had never been a vocabulary word, but I could guess what it meant. Feeble. "That's right, Mom. Great-Grandpa looked terrible at breakfast. He was so shaky he could hardly—"

Sophie didn't let me finish. "By amenable, I mean Lester is more willing to listen to reason, Kimball. As for his health, he don't ever sleep well. He'll spruce up by midday, I promise. Why, he's prob'ly dozing on the Bridge now."

"Then I'll wait till later to speak to him," Mom said. "But as for fixing up the house, how can we ever do it in a morning? Can't the Realtor wait a few days?"

"No, Doug's made all his plans to come out today. He travels a lot, and there's no telling when he can get over again." Sophie was commander in chief and not about to let anyone forget it.

Poor Mom. She's pretty good as a handyman. She can sew almost anything out of flowered sheets and add potted plants in all the right places. But there was no way she could tackle The Anchorage and have it in any kind of shape even if she worked a month. If nothing else, she was a good sport, and I could see her mentally roll up her sleeves, the blue and white china forgotten. For now.

Even after we started working I didn't have a chance to talk to Mom alone. General Sophie assigned me all the windows to wash on the inside while Mom washed on the outside. For such a dark house, how could there be so many windows? Still, with the living room draperies open and the windows clean, the place did look better. At least brighter. And the fog was lifting. It was like a curtain going up on a lighted stage. As I finished one window and went on to the next, it was as if my washing were brightening the house and not just the sun coming out.

I climbed the stairs to the landing and pulled back the draperies. And groaned. The four landing windows were huge. And divided into little panes. I stood up on the wide windowsill and started spraying. As soon as I had cleaned one full window, I looked out. I still couldn't see the water. Or the beach where the boy had hidden his boat.

By the time I finished all four windows my arms were ready to drop off. And it was hard to balance so long on the wide window ledge. I leaned back against the paneling beside the window to rest a minute. Without warning, the whole panel collapsed under me. If I hadn't grabbed the draperies, I would have fallen off the windowsill.

Good night, now what had I done? I turned around and looked at the panel. It hadn't so much broken as sort of swung into the wall. No wood had splintered, and nothing seemed out of place. In fact, it looked as if it were meant to open. I stuck my head in the opening. Gingerly. Who knew what might be in there? It was dark and musty, all right, but nothing alive leaped out at me. The opening went deep into the wall and was lined with shelves. The top shelves were crammed with piles of letters tied into bundles. Yellow newspapers and long rolls of dull blue paper were stacked on the bottom shelves. I pulled out a bundle of letters. The top envelope had been ripped in half so I could read only part of the address:

Mrs. Enos R. Ki
Old Bridge Ro
Watoset, Mai
United State

I flipped through the rest of the letters. Every envelope had been torn, and every envelope was addressed to Mrs. Enos R. Ki. It must be Kimball. But who was Mrs. Enos

R. Kimball? Maybe there were more papers behind the panel on the other side of the windows.

There were. When I pushed the upper part of the second panel, it swung in just like the first. Two secret panels! The shelves behind the second panel were full of worn black notebooks and big leather scrapbooks.

Really excited now, I opened the top notebook to the first page. "Written by Enos R. Kimball—age 15—Boy— [or ordinary seaman] on the ship *Sam Sturges*," it read. "A story of my adventures in China to be read by the dear folks at home by and bye. Diary of my trip to Shanghai, China & Singapore. Began April 23, 1882, and Ended on March 17, 1883."

Enos R. Kimball must have been my great-great-grand-father, and these notebooks were his diaries. Eighteen eighty-two was a hundred twenty-five years ago! I looked down at the book in my hands. Roots. That's what having roots meant. "To be read by the dear folks at home by and bye." That was me. Great-Grandpa and Mom and I were all that was left of the dear folks at home. At the thought, sudden tears filled my eyes and blurred the fine spidery handwriting on the page in front of me.

EIGHT

A Treasury
of Memories

I leafed through a few pages of the first notebook. It was a diary, just like the one I got on my tenth birthday. But Great-Great-Grandfather had done better than I had. I quit after a month, and it looked as if he had kept a diary for years.

What was in the scrapbooks? They smelled moldy, and the leather had crumbled. Photograph albums, that's what they were. The first album had pictures of ladies in wide-brimmed hats and long dresses. The mustached men wore straw hats and white slacks. "Gladys, Oscar, Maude, Warren, Fanny." Smiling, long-ago people.

"Come in, Doug. I knew you'd be over soon's the fog lifted." Sophie's voice echoed up the stairs from the hall below.

I heard a man's mumbled reply. Then Sophie spoke again. Her voice carried like a drill sergeant's. "Best you stay clear of the Bridge, Doug. Lester's not feeling up to snuff."

I peered down from the landing but couldn't see either Sophie or Doug whatever-his-name-was. Good, that meant they couldn't see me either. Not that I was doing anything wrong, I told myself, but I just didn't want Sophie to find me poking around. Their conversation disappeared into the dining room.

I settled down on the windowsill to read, more excited than if I had found the panels filled with gold coins. "April 22, 1882. Today I arrived in New York by Fall River Line Steamer. Straightaway I found my way to the wharf & got my first view of the *Sam Sturges*. She is trim in appearance with long, tapering spars. All my regrets are swept away. I feel I have made no mistake in adopting a sailor's life." I read on. And on.

"Kimball!" Mom shouted right in my ear. "Didn't you hear me call you, young lady? I need your help outside."

The fact is, I hadn't heard her. When I really get into something, I don't register at all. One time I was reading a Harry Potter book in the school library when there was a fire drill. I never even heard the alarm go off. And no one missed me. I might have burned to death for all any-one cared.

"Oh, Mom, look what I found. Secret panels by the win-dows, all full of stuff like diaries and letters and albums." I slid off the windowsill and pointed to my discovery.

"Here, let me see." Mom put down her bucket of soapy water and pulled off her rubber gloves. She glanced through the top album and notebook. Then she pushed the panels back and forth a few times. She stuck her head in like I had and pulled out the long rolls of blue paper. She spread them on the windowsill. They were old blueprints of the house.

"The Anchorage, Shag Island, Maine, 1925," she read aloud. "All these things are really fantastic, Kim. But they belong to Grandpa, and you must ask him if you can look through them."

I knew she was right. Diaries are diaries, and letters are letters, no matter how old. Mom and I have a pact not to read each other's mail. Which isn't really fair. Mom gets all sorts of interesting-looking letters, and I never get anything but a kiddie magazine my godmother still gives me for Christmas.

"If I ask Great-Grandpa now, will you come with me, Mom?"

"Sure." She agreed so fast I knew she was curious, too.

I picked up some diaries, letters, and the blueprints, while Mom put everything else back on the shelves. Just as we started down the stairs, a man came out of the dining room. He was tall, with wavy gray hair and a good tan. He wore glasses and was very handsome.

"Well, good morning." His great smile showed big white teeth. I always notice teeth because mine aren't so great. My friend Sarah always notices legs. That's because her teeth are fine, but her legs are fat.

He stuck out his hand to Mom. "You must be Margaret

Kimball. It's nice to meet you. I'm Doug Tate." I was surprised when Bert told me you were here. Stunned, you might say. I've been out of town, so hadn't heard you were coming."

"I'm glad to meet you, too, Mr. Tate. Actually, I'm Margaret Lauder now. And this is my daughter, Kimball." Mom has class all right. She was dressed like a cleaning woman, but pulled off the introductions as if she were in evening clothes.

"Maybe Sophie told you I'm handling The Anchorage for Uncle Lester." Mr. Tate took out a pack of cigarettes and offered one to Mom. To my disgust, they both lit up. "I have a potential buyer who's interested in The Anchorage as a hotel."

"No doubt Grandpa will have something to say about that," Mom commented dryly. "But you call him Uncle Lester. Are you and Grandpa related?"

"Not really. My great-great-uncle Alfred and Lester's father were close friends. Uncle Alfred built most of these big old mausoleums around here called cottages. The Anchorage was his pièce de résistance."

Mom laughed. "He built them and you sell them. That's a twist. Maybe his picture is in one of these albums Kim has here."

Mr. Tate focused on me for the first time. "Oh, what's that, Kim?"

"Old diaries and letters and blueprints I just found," I bragged, pointing back toward the landing.

Mr. Tate seemed startled. He frowned and stepped forward with his hand out, as if to ask for them. Then he stopped, took a long drag on his cigarette, and smiled. "I didn't know anything like that was in The Anchorage. Old Enos Kimball was quite a man. Even with his mind gone at the end with all that Chinese ghost nonsense, he was still remarkable."

Mom sat down on the bottom step. "My great-grandfather always scared me half to death. Still, I only knew him in his last years. . . ."

They sounded as if they were going to hash out the whole family tree. And I was dying to get started on the diaries. "Mom, I'm going to ask Great-Grandpa about these things?" I made it sound like a question so she'd remember she was going with me.

No one is sharper than Mom when she wants to be. But sometimes she doesn't want. "Fine, he's on the Bridge." She turned back to Mr. Tate. "It's funny to think that Grandpa is the same age now that—"

There was no point hanging around. I headed for the living room and the Bridge door at the end of it. A grunt from inside answered my knock. I opened the door. Great-Grandpa was reading his newspaper.

"Hello," I said.

But Great-Grandpa didn't answer or look up. Now that I was in the lion's den, I wasn't sure I even had the nerve to show Great-Grandpa what I had found, let alone ask him if I could look through it all. I watched him read his paper for a minute, then I walked over to the window. I gasped. The fog was gone, and there was a whole rock full of seals not far from shore.

"Wow. I've been waiting to see seals since I got here." But it was hard to separate one seal from another. Their gray blended into the water and the rocks. I put the diaries and albums and blueprints on a chair and pressed against the window to see better.

"You want to look through the 'scope at the seals?" Great-Grandpa asked curtly. "Glasses, *humph*. Take 'em off, and we'll see what we can do."

He showed me how to focus the telescope. I turned the knob. A blurry boat jumped in front of me, then the seal rock. Another turn, and the seals were as clear as the picture on a plasma TV. One seal slid off into the water. Another followed. Lots of them seemed to be asleep.

"What's all this?" I turned around. Great-Grandpa was holding the stack of letters and books. "This is Father's writing. These are Father's logs. Where did you get them?"

"I found them in the two panels by the landing windows." Maybe he had forgotten they were there. Or hadn't known.

He took two steps back and dropped into his chair. Collapsed was more like it. "All these years I never knew where they were."

I felt like a thief. "I leaned on the panel, and it just opened up. There's lots more stuff."

Great-Grandpa untied the string around the letters.

His hands trembled as he slid one out and looked at it. "These are Father's letters to Mother and us children when he was away. I thought they had been lost forever. . . . Father spent forty-three years at sea. When they were first married, Mother traveled with him, and we children were born on shipboard, Gwen in the Atlantic, Warren in the Indian Ocean, and me in the South China Sea."

Even I had the sense to know he was talking to himself and not to me. Oral history, that's what this was. I hardly dared breathe as I slid into the chair next to his.

"Once, on Mother's birthday, Father sailed into Hong Kong Harbor and raised all his flags, a hundred or more from the bowsprit to the stern. Pretty soon all the other American ships in the harbor raised their flags, too. Father said it was a beautiful sight. Later, on shore, at the American consul, the other shipmasters asked Father about the celebration. They'd been at sea two or three years and thought there was a new American holiday since they'd left the United States."

"Why, Kimball, I didn't know you were out here." The spell was broken. It was Sophie's booming voice and Sophie's big body filling the doorway. "I just came to tell Lester that Doug Tate's—what are those?" She stepped into the room and stood staring down at the letters and notebooks. "Why, those . . . where did you find them? They . . . I . . . ." she sputtered. Her face flushed, and her short gray hair seemed to stand on end as if an electrical current had gone right through her.

NINE

A Silent Docking

"Those letters . . ." Sophie stammered again. Then she took a deep breath like I do to pull myself together. "I thought you said all those things were lost, Lester."

"Lost and then found." Great-Grandpa raised his salt-and-pepper eyebrows. "And who do you think found them? This young lady . . . uh . . . Kimball." He turned to me and laughed. It was the first time I ever heard him laugh, and it was a nice, rumbling chuckle. "Can you imagine? I almost couldn't come up with your name. Anyway, Kimball here found Father's old letters. The envelopes are ripped, but the letters 'pear intact."

Sophie stared at the letters as Great-Grandpa slipped them into his sweater pocket. She looked like me in front of a bubble-gum machine. Frustrated. I was glad Great-Grandpa hadn't mentioned where I found them. And even gladder Mom had put everything else back and closed the panels.

"I came out to tell you that Bert . . . I mean Doug Tate is here about the . . . I mean, the house." Sophie's tongue tripped over her words. "You recall, I told you that Doug was coming."

Great-Grandpa stood up so fast he surprised me. He came only to Sophie's shoulder, but she took a startled step back. I knew how she felt. There was something formidable about Great-Grandpa in spite of his size. "You have told me, Sophie. And told me. And told me. Now I'm going to tell you something." He tapped his finger on the table. "Doug Tate's a nice enough fella. As a friend he's welcome. But as a house seller, he's not. Now I want you to keep him out of my sight."

I expected a barrage of protest from Sophie. But she must have known when she was bested. She stalked out with a loud *humph.*

Great-Grandpa humphed, too. "That Sophie. *Humph.*" He was mad, but he seemed brighter than he had at breakfast, and I was encouraged. I opened the photograph album.

"Who's this, Great-Grandpa?" I asked, pointing to the first page. "Gwen, Louise, Fanny. Swanton Beach, Summer, 1924." Two of the women held on to their hats. The third held a birdcage.

Great-Grandpa studied the picture. "Gwen was my sister, and Louise Benton was our cousin. They're both gone now. And Fanny." He chuckled his nice chuckle. "Fanny Tillis worked for Mother twenty-six years. When she was with us in Watoset, she fell in love with a ship rigger.

Riggers used to travel around, rigging ships after they were built. When the job was done, the rigger left town. He and Fanny used to correspond, but since Fanny couldn't read or write, I wrote all her letters for her. I must have been about twelve. She'd tell me what to write; then I'd improve on it some. I was a regular Cupid. See the bird Fanny's holding? Father always brought back a tropical bird—usually a parrot—from his trips, and Fanny was great shakes at training those birds. Fanny was like family, but she ended up at the poor farm. Humiliating, that's what the poor farm is."

There were as many pictures of the stocky little Fanny as there were of anyone else, usually with a birdcage in her hand or a bird perched on her shoulder. So many people in so many pictures, and Great-Grandpa could remember them all. Aunts, uncles, cousins, friends, even dogs. He had the best memory of just about anyone I ever met.

Two whole pages of pictures were of a family clambake. Great-Grandpa told me exactly how they steamed their clams and corn in seaweed over hot rocks. "Lobsters? Never recall having one as a boy. They were too expensive, twenty-five cents a pound, where a milk quart of clams only cost fifteen cents. They used to ship lobsters in ice to Boston by train."

"Is there a picture of your father?" I asked, then could have kicked myself. I didn't want to wreck Great-Grandpa's good mood.

But he took off his glasses and leaned back in his chair.

"The simple fact is, Father was never home long enough to be photographed. When he had the Liverpool to San Francisco run around Cape Horn, he was away four years. Then there was the time he was captured by Chinese pirates off Hainan. They lured Father's ship up on the rocks with false lights. He was gone a good while then." Great-Grandpa paused. "But Father never liked to talk about that experience. Anyways, until he retired, the most we'd see him would be ten days. Then he'd be off again for a year or more. When he retired, he built this place, The Anchorage. A ship comes into harbor and drops her anchor. Father came home and dropped his anchor. But he never got over the sea. The Bridge, here, was his room. See, that's his barometer and steering compass and speaking trumpet and telescope."

Great-Grandpa stood up and, leaning on his cane, pointed out all the instruments to me. "Here's his sextant and chronometer. The captain shoots the stars with the sextant as the chronometer gives the exact time. It takes some elaborate figuring to get the longitude and latitude of the ship."

He raised his cane toward a large oil painting. "For two dollars fifty cents, a Chinese painter in Canton rowed out and painted Father's ship. Being tied up, all the sags were set. But the Chinaman knew how every sail looked and painted them in as accurate as you please."

I looked more closely at the painting. Mounted on the bow was a statue of a woman holding something in her hands, flowers or a book. It was almost like the statue by the fireplace. A figurehead, that's what it was. And I was the dummy not to have realized it.

"Ayuh, who's there?" Great-Grandpa called out.

I hadn't even heard the knock, so was surprised to see Mom come in. I was even more surprised to see her in linen pants and a silk shirt. She looked strictly twenty-first century, and I was still in the twentieth. "Doug Tate hasn't finished yet, but Sophie wants to go ahead with dinner. We'll eat in ten minutes," she said.

Great-Grandpa pulled out a pocket watch. "One thirty! What's got into Sophie that our noon-dinner is so late? That woman is showing her age, I tell you." He was his old grumpy self. Now I knew him better I didn't mind at all.

I left the Bridge before Mom and Great-Grandpa. I wanted to be alone for a minute. I headed out the front door and walked to the edge of the cliff where the stairs started down to the dock. What a beautiful view. No wonder Enos Kimball had wanted to build his anchorage here. Only the tops of the pine trees stirred in the light breeze. Far away, sailboats drifted in slow motion while gulls circled overhead like lookouts. Then I saw a motor-boat cut a V-shaped path through the water toward our dock. It looked like the *Lucky Sue,* but I couldn't be sure. Besides, Bert had said he always rang his bell three times when he approached our landing.

It was the *Lucky Sue.* Bert docked her, and I saw Roger jump out. But that was funny. Bert never rang his bell at all. Mom would probably be disappointed he'd arrived. She had gotten all dressed up for Mr. Tate, and now it was time for him to leave. I guess I couldn't blame her. Mr. Tate *was* good-looking.

I watched Roger head for the cliff steps, a big carton in his arms. I could see just the top of his head zig in one direction, then zag in another until he reached the top. And me.

"Greetings," he said. He didn't act surprised to see me. But he was pretty cool anyway, as if not much ever surprised him.

"Hi, did you come for Mr. Tate?" Chalk up another brilliant Kimball Lauder remark.

"Yeah. And this order from Sears arrived for Sophie." Roger gave the carton a shake. "I don't know what it could be. That house is so full of junk now you can hardly get in it."

"That's not junk. Those are valuable family heirlooms." I'd changed my tune. Mom had said things would look different in the morning, and they did.

"Huh, those old moose antlers heirlooms? That's news. Maybe this is something valuable, too, like another hat rack." Roger laughed all the way into the house.

"Humph." I understood why Great-Grandpa and Sophie humphed. It was very satisfying.

As I turned to follow Roger, I sensed, rather than saw, a quick motion on the rocks below. I moved to the top step and looked down. Someone was approaching the dock by a narrow path along the cliff ledge. It was an out-cropping of rock just wide enough to walk on more than a real path. I sucked in my breath. The same blond boy with the ponytail I had seen earlier on the cove beach ran down the dock ramp. He jumped aboard the *Lucky Sue.*

Good, I thought, he's going back to Watoset, and that will be the end of him. He's just summer people like Sophie said. But then I saw the boy climb out of the *Lucky Sue* carrying a duffel bag. Bert followed him. They shook hands. Then, as Bert reboarded his boat, the boy started back up the dock ramp toward shore. Something must have caught his eye, maybe the sun reflecting off my glasses. He stopped and looked up at the cliff staircase. And at me. There I was, with no place to hide, as plain to see as the figurehead on a ship. The boy glared at me for a long moment, then hurried the rest of the way up the ramp. His duffel bag bumped against his legs as he turned left by the water's edge. I watched him run along the narrow ledge until a stand of spruce trees cut him from my view.

TEN

A Command Call

As soon as the blond boy was out of sight, I had to go to the bathroom. I ran back to the house. Mom and Mr. Tate and Roger were in the front hall. Only Mom didn't give me a funny look as I shot past them up the stairs.

By the time I came back down, they were gone. I was just as glad. When Mom returned, we could talk alone. I started to pace the hall waiting for her. Though my dad has always been a pacer, I had never tried it. I was surprised to find it helped. Up and down, back and forth, faster and faster.

Mom opened the front door. It sounds corny, but her eyes sparkled. She pulled a pack of cigarettes from her pocket and lit one. "Well, Cousin Doug turned out to be quite a pleasant surprise." She tilted her head and raised her eyebrows.

It was her way of getting my opinion without really

asking. Any other time I would have been glad to discuss it. But not now. I pulled her over behind the stairs in case Sophie was around. "Listen, Mom, there's a boy on this island. Bert knows he's here, and I think Sophie does, too. He's got a boat. The worst of it is, he saw me see him."

Mom laughed. "Whoa, Dobbin. What are you talking about?"

I told her the whole story. Slowly.

"Margaret, is that a cigarette?" I hadn't noticed Great-Grandpa come into the front hall from the living room. Neither had Mom. We both jumped.

"Why . . . yes, it is," Mom stammered,

"I never permitted your father to smoke, and there's no reason why I should tolerate it from you," Great-Grandpa said tartly.

"I'm not a child, Grandpa, and smoking gives me pleasure." Mom was smiling, but her voice was as tart as his.

"Some might reckon driving a hundred miles an hour gives 'em pleasure, too," Great-Grandpa retorted.

Two identical pairs of blue eyes met. Mom dropped hers first. She grinned sheepishly and put out her cigarette in a china dish. I couldn't help grinning myself. Great-Grandpa must have noticed. He winked at me. It was the same quick wink as the night before. Only this time I knew I'd really seen it.

"Noon-dinner's late," he snapped. He headed for the kitchen.

"We'll talk about it later, honey," Mom whispered to me.

After we'd worked our way through Sophie's roast chicken, mashed potatoes, and gravy dinner, we cleaned up. Then Mom and I went outside and sat on the front steps.

"I'm quite certain there's no other house on Shag Island," Mom began.

I shook my head. "There isn't. Sophie claims he's just some kid hanging around. But I think she knew he was here all along. And Bert knows for sure. He gave the boy a duffel bag."

"I can't say it sounds very serious." Mom pulled out her cigarettes and started to light one. Then she blew out her match. "Honestly, isn't Grandpa something, not allowing me to smoke?" But the way she said it I knew she admired him. Maybe that's because she's stubborn herself.

I could be stubborn, too. "What about the boy?"

"I tell you what, Kim. After that chicken dinner, I could use some exercise. I feel absolutely bloated. Suppose we go for a walk around the island and see if that boy turns up."

As it worked out, Mom and I had a fantastic afternoon. In our bathing suits and sneakers, we covered every inch of shoreline. And we found no sign of the blond boy. Not one. Not even a footprint in the sand like Robinson Crusoe. There was no duffel bag and no boat. He had picked up his duffel bag and taken off in his motorboat, that's what Mom decided. I agreed. Maybe I agreed because Mom and I were having such a good time.

We spent the afternoon exploring the tidepools, each

one different with barnacles, starfish, mussels, and tiny crabs that scurried sideways when we stirred up the water. We slipped and slid on the seaweed that swayed under the surface like knotted witch's hair. We sat on the rocks and watched the seabirds. We even found a rickety boat on the cove beach and went rowing. But it leaked so much and so fast we barely made it back to shore before swamping. Mom is a good swimmer, but I can barely stay afloat. And the water off the beach was deep.

I never thought I'd be hungry again, but when Sophie put down baked beans and brown bread for supper at five o'clock, I ate a whole plateful. And I'm not a baked bean fan.

"Even on shipboard Father demanded beans on Saturday night," Great-Grandpa commented.

"Your father was a very demanding man," Sophie said.

"He didn't ask for more than he gave. He was a good shipmaster and never lost a ship." But Great-Grandpa didn't say what kind of father he had been. Certainly an absent one. Like mine. Every year I saw Dad less and less. Sometimes he took me with him on vacations, first with Lisa, his second wife, then with Sharon, his third. But they had kids of their own, and I hated the confusion of stepbrothers and sisters and babysitters to get straightened out. This was my kind of vacation.

And for the next ten days it was. Every morning Mom and I worked on The Anchorage. We even went to Watoset in the *Lucky Sue* to buy fabric for curtains. Mom stitched away on Sophie's ancient sewing machine while I painted trim. We dusted and scrubbed. I took on the figureheads as my special project. By the time I had washed them and touched up their bare spots with fresh paint they were old friends.

During Great-Grandpa's afternoon nap Mom and I hiked around the island. We went wading and sunbathed. We got tan and fat. At least Mom got tan, and I got fat. I even felt like I was beginning to get some shape. I was no supermodel, but it was a start.

When Great-Grandpa woke up from his nap, the two of us read over the old diaries and looked at the albums while he told me wonderful stories. Then I came up with the idea to record Great-Grandpa as he talked. I'd turned on the old radio Sophie had given me just to see if it worked, and noticed a Record button for tapes. When I told Mom what I wanted to do, she gave Roger money to buy some tapes in Watoset so that I could record Great-Grandpa's stories.

And Great-Grandpa was ham enough to enjoy it. "Shags are those black birds with the long necks. They're really cormorants, but everyone in these parts calls them shags," Great-Grandpa explained when I asked him how the island got its name. "They're greedy birds, gluttons you might say. In China they're used for fishing. Their owners band their throats so the birds can't swallow. Then they're let out on the end of a long line. After the shags fill their throats with fish, they're pulled back to the boat and forced to give up their catch. Shags were almost extinct around here eighty years or so ago, but they're coming back in good numbers. I like to watch them. Sitting on the cliffs drying their wings, they look like rows of black bottles."

And they did. But then I enjoyed watching *all* the birds through the telescope. And the seals, too. When we tired of recording, Great-Grandpa and I played dominoes. Great-Grandpa didn't just like to win. He loved to win. Hard as I tried, he beat me fair and square almost every game. During that time neither of us talked about selling The Anchorage. Somehow we both knew it would break the magic spell.

Great-Grandpa began to look better. His eyes were brighter, and his hands steadier. And he said he had been sleeping more soundly than he had in months. After the first couple of nights in The Anchorage, I slept better, too. My second night I had stayed awake a long time, just waiting for the Chinese chimes to begin. But they never came. On the third night Great-Grandpa had read to us from his newspaper about meteor showers expected that evening. Mom and I had lain out on the dock until one o'clock in the morning, watching fantastic shooting stars burst across the clear sky. After that I never thought about the Chinese music again.

And of all things, Roger Coombs turned out to be unexpected fun. Our friendship started the day Mom and I went to Watoset in the *Lucky Sue*. On the dock I had been horsing around and fell off. Roger howled. That made me furious. But when he threw a perfect shot with a life preserver right over my head like a doughnut, I had to laugh, too.

Then, on Roger's next day off, Mom hired him to come out and cut down some heavy brush. I worked with him most of the day, and we had a ball. We found a bees' nest in a hollow tree and Roger smoked out the bees. It was the most exciting/terrifying thing I ever saw. But the honey was delicious.

At the end of ten days I hated to think our vacation was almost half over. I woke that Monday morning to a heavy fog. Being an old Down Easter by now, I was sure it would lift before mid-morning. Not that I wanted it to. At eleven Mr. Tate was bringing out his clients to look over The Anchorage.

When I came downstairs for breakfast, Mom and Great-Grandpa and Sophie were in the dining room by the radio. They were hovering over it, looking so much like underground spies in a World War II movie that I almost burst out laughing. Luckily I didn't.

"I just can't imagine who would be trying to reach me." Mom sounded worried.

There was a crackling from the set. Then Bert's voice came over, his Maine accent exaggerated by the static. "K1XXX, this is W1ZZY. I'm putting you through on the phone patch with the call for Margaret Lauder."

Great-Grandpa tapped Mom on the shoulder. "Just say 'over' when you're finished talking, so Bert can switch from transmit to receive."

Mom nodded, looking nervous.

There was a pause. Then, "Hello there, Maggie-pie. Can you hear me? It's Harvey here."

Oh, brother, it was Mom's boss, Harvey Pastori. Mr. Harvey, the interior designer. I always call him Have-a-pastrami.

"I never thought I'd get through to you. Where are you, up with the Eskimos? Over."

I was embarrassed. Great-Grandpa and Sophie stood by the set listening. Even Dash looked alert.

Mom was embarrassed, too. "Of course not, Harvey. What is it? Over."

"A crisis, Maggie, what else? Mrs. La Bronquist is hysterical. The wrong rug came. Two lamps arrived broken. Her bedroom came out a poisonous blue. You'll just have to come down and cope. Over."

I hadn't thought of Harvey for so long he sounded like he was speaking a foreign language. Mom must have thought so, too.

"It's out of the question, Harvey. I'm on an island. Over."

"But it's all arranged. I've made plane reservations for you and Kim tonight on the eight o'clock flight from Portland. You can meet with La Bronquist in the A.M., pacify her, and be back up there by Wednesday night. Over."

Mom looked back at me and raised her eyebrows.

I shrugged. We didn't have to discuss it. Harvey knew what he wanted, and he wanted Mom in New York. And Mom needed her job.

"All right, Harvey. If it's only until Wednesday, Kim and I will be down. Over."

"I promise. Not a minute more. Over."

Mom stood up to let Great-Grandpa sign off. She sighed. "What a rotten shame, Kim, dragging you back to New York. But you know Harvey. For all his silly ways, he's a tyrant."

"I don't see any point in me even going, Mom. I can stay here. I'll take a vacation from cleaning and just get fat on Sophie's cooking."

I had been trying to get along better with Sophie. I turned to speak to her, but she was gone. I saw just the edge of her apron as she rushed around the corner of the dining room into the kitchen.

ELEVEN

The Departure

The rest of the morning was confusion. With Mr. Tate due at eleven with his clients, Mom had planned to weed and clip the front yard. Instead, she spent the time packing and going over Mrs. La Bronquist's plans.

"If only there were a phone, I could check with the painter . . . the rug man . . . make sure I can get a car to Portland . . ." She was getting tenser and tenser. I could have kicked Harvey for spoiling our vacation. "Maybe you should come to New York with me after all, Kim," she said for the fifth time. She planned to return to Watoset in the *Lucky Sue,* then rent a car for the drive to Portland.

"It's only for two days. Great-Grandpa and I will be fine. And Sophie will be here," I reassured her.

"I guess so." Mrs. La Bronquist had given Mom a hard time for months. And Harvey had sounded really annoyed. "Anyway, do me a favor, will you, Kim? Trim around the front yard before Doug gets here. Make it look neat."

"If The Anchorage gets sold, what will happen to Great-Grandpa? Will he go to the poor farm like Fanny Tillis?"

Mom stopped packing and looked at me, a long look. "Oh, Kimmy, where did you get such an idea? Grandpa won't go to the poor farm. There isn't even such a thing anymore. He has a pension and Social Security, and with what he gets for this house, he can buy a nice little place in Watoset. And you know The Anchorage is in his name. If he doesn't want to sell it, he doesn't have to."

Mom just didn't understand how Great-Grandpa felt. It was easy enough to say he didn't have to sell. But what if he got sick? Mom didn't realize that Great-Grandpa was cross all the time because he was so worried. But I couldn't go into all that when Mom was so uptight herself.

"I guess I'll do the front yard," I said instead.

The sun was the hottest since we had arrived. There was always a breeze up by the house, but as I started to clip, the air was as thick as soup. I had never clipped before. In half an hour blisters began to bubble on my palms. My glasses got all steamed up, and my hair frizzed into one giant kink.

Just as I finished clipping by the porch, I heard the *Lucky Sue*'s bell. I laid the clippers on the porch and headed for the cliff stairs. We had worked out a regular pony express relay team. Minus the horses. When Bert arrived, I met the *Lucky Sue* to pick up Great-Grandpa's mail and newspaper. By the time I got back up the cliff stairs Sophie was waiting on the porch to take them in to Great-Grandpa. Post office to Bert, Bert to me, me to Sophie, Sophie to Great-Grandpa. Like it was all urgent mail, instead of just bills and junk mail and stuff.

Anyway, I had ulterior, or maybe interior was a better word, motives for meeting the *Lucky Sue*. Roger Coombs was the only person I ever saw who was my age. Sarah would probably have made a big deal out of it, but there was nothing going on between Roger and me. We were just good friends. Roger knew every kind of bird, animal, fish, and crustacean there was, and he pointed them all out to me. We had big arguments on how squirrels and chipmunks and even bees had got to Shag Island in the first place. Roger said they had swum over or flown over or hiked a ride on a boat. I claimed they had been on the island from the beginning, before it separated from the mainland. Roger liked to argue about everything. So did I.

"I'll get the mail today, Kimball," I heard Sophie shout as I started for the cliff stairs. I turned around. Sophie was charging down the path. "I have to see Bert. He's got a package for me." Her face was redder than ever.

I looked down at the dock. Mr. Tate and three men were climbing out of the *Lucky Sue*. I didn't see Roger. If Roger wasn't there, I might as well save myself the trip.

As Sophie headed down the stairs, I studied the men below. Mr. Tate wore a sports jacket and a polo shirt, as Brooks Brothers sharp as ever. But my heart sank at the sight of the other men. They all wore business suits as grim as funeral directors. In the back of my mind, I had imagined a nice young couple in jeans who would fall in love with The Anchorage and let Great-Grandpa live on with them. But these executive types looked about as warm as Sophie's day-old popovers.

Mr. Tate reached the top of the stairs first. He was carrying a big camera case. "Morning, Kim," he said. He wasn't even out of breath as he introduced the men who were huffing and puffing their way up behind him. "Kim, I'd like you to meet Mr. Croft, Mr. Schaeffer, and Mr. Murray. Gentlemen, this is Mr. Kimball's great-granddaughter, Kimball Lauder."

He was really smooth. I could be smooth, too. "Hi." I smiled at the three men.

It couldn't have mattered less. They hardly noticed me. The first man wiped his sweaty face with a big handkerchief, and the other two were breathless and wheezing. They all carried briefcases. "That's quite a climb for guests with luggage," one man said.

"It could be graded some," Mr. Tate answered. "And if people want an island retreat, they like to feel they're roughing it a bit."

They really did mean business.

The men paced off the front yard, studied the house, and looked back over the bay. Why did that fog have to clear? The view with the bright sun glinting off the water had never been so dazzling. My paint job had jazzed up the whole front entrance. Even my clipping had helped.

One of the men clapped Mr. Tate on the back. "You didn't kid us with your sales pitch, Douglas. This looks like a real possibility."

"I'll get interior shots first, then some of this view and the exterior," Mr. Tate said, and they all headed for the house.

Just as they started up the steps, Mom came out the front door. She looked great, New York great with a Maine tan. She had on a yellow-and-blue dress with a blue scarf that just matched her eyes. I could tell she was a surprise by the way the three men straightened up. She shook hands all around. Then, with a murmured apology, she drew Mr. Tate over to where I was standing.

"Grandpa is acting up, Doug. He locked himself on the Bridge and won't open the door."

I mentally cheered. A one-person protest was Great-Grandpa's best chance.

"Thanks for the warning, Margaret. I'll stay clear of the Bridge, and maybe Kim can entertain Uncle Lester for the time being." Mr. Tate nodded at me before he turned back to Mom. "We should be through in a couple of hours if you two want to count on one o'clock as launch time, Margaret. Your going back with us in the *Lucky Sue* just might clinch the deal."

"I'm not sure I'd be so pleased at that, but you do flatter me, Cousin Doug," Mom said. She squeezed my arm. "Keep up Grandpa's spirits, will you, Kimmy?"

I stood where I was by the cliff stairs while everyone, including Mom, went into the house. Mom must have been out to lunch. Didn't she register on the fact Mr. Tate knew she was going back to the mainland? And thought I was going, too? Why, Bert must have repeated Mom's whole conversation with Harvey to Mr. Tate. That had to be against the law, like wiretapping!

I looked down at the dock. Bert and Sophie stood by the boat talking. Then Bert handed Sophie a big picnic basket. He put his arm around her and gave her a hug. He was so small and she was so big, any other time, I would have laughed. But not now. Bert Smith was a real sleaze. Furious, I stomped back into the house.

Though I hated to be in on a plot to keep Great-Grandpa distracted, I was glad to spend the morning with him. Knowing he didn't have to sell The Anchorage unless he wanted to was the only reason I didn't feel like a sleaze myself. We played dominoes for what seemed hours. Then Great-Grandpa dozed off in his chair, his dime-store glasses still on his nose and his newspaper open on his lap. Asleep that way, he looked very, very old. And helpless too, like a sleeping baby.

"*Sst*, Kim," Mom called to me through the locked door.

I slipped out of the room. There was no need to wake Great-Grandpa.

"We're leaving now. Doug is driving his clients to the Portland Airport and can take me, too. Isn't that lucky?"

Mr. Tate and the three men were waiting on the dock for Mom. Bert had already started up the *Lucky Sue*'s motor by the time we reached them. The men were talking about elevators and telephone lines and more bath-rooms. *Go home! Forget it!* I felt like yelling.

"Kim, honey, are you sure you'll be all right?" Mom asked as Mr. Tate helped her into the *Lucky Sue*.

Mr. Tate looked up. "Aren't you coming, too, Kim?" He seemed surprised.

I shook my head. "I decided to stay here." All of a sudden I wasn't so thrilled with the idea. But what could I do? If I told Mom I didn't want her to leave, I knew she would hop right out of the boat and not go to New York at all. And that wasn't fair. Darn that Harvey Pastori anyway.

Bert turned the wheel, and the *Lucky Sue* swung out into the water. Mom stood in the stern and waved. The air was still. The water was still. Everything seemed to hang in hot silence. Even the gulls didn't squawk and screech. They hovered, too, dipping and gliding like white kites on a string. Only the chug of the boat's motor vibrated back to me, fainter and fainter. When I could no longer see Mom's bright yellow dress in the stern, I started back up to the house.

As I headed up the stairs, my attention was caught by a quick movement beyond the cliff rocks. It looked like a mop of blond hair. The world stopped. No, it was only a squirrel running across the ledge. But my heart wasn't so logical. It kept thumping in my chest. I hadn't realized that blond boy was still so much on my mind. A finger of sweat started at my armpit and crept wetly down my skin as I climbed the rest of the way to the top.

TWELVE

An Emergency

I glanced up at The Anchorage. If I squinted, its gray ells and wings looked like a huge out-of-shape elephant. Somehow I just didn't feel like going inside, especially with Great-Grandpa asleep, and Sophie . . . who knew where Sophie was? I hadn't seen her since she and Bert had been talking on the dock hours ago.

Mom was to be gone for only two and a half days. That wasn't long. It only seemed long. I sat down on the porch steps and sighed. I hate sighers. But sometimes a *humph* helps, and sometimes a sigh helps. A sigh now felt just right. I pushed up my shorts as far as they would go and stretched out my legs. They weren't any tanner than when I had arrived, only frecklier. If ever I was going to tan, this was the day. The sun was a hot ball in the sky. A big gull dozed on the cliff stair railing, its yellow bill tucked under its feathers. I took off my glasses and closed my eyes, too.

But the sun wasn't tanning me. It was steaming me like a green lobster turning red. Sweat popped out over my lip in a wet mustache. I opened my eyes and put my glasses back on. The gull hadn't moved a feather. Maybe immobility was the answer. But I couldn't stay still that long. I said the word "immobility" aloud, stringing it out. I'd learned it last year but never used it. I sighed again. I might as well go in the house. At least the house was cool.

It was cool, all right, but this afternoon, it seemed gloomier than ever. Maybe that was because I felt so gloomy myself. I headed for the kitchen. Sophie's big meals must have stretched my stomach. I was hungry all the time.

Sophie sat at the kitchen table peeling carrots, just as if she'd been there all day. She looked up at me and nodded. I nodded back, not certain what to say. Meat was cooking with a tomatoey smell. Stew, that's what Sophie was cooking. Only two o'clock, and supper was already started. I was used to Mom, who dashed in at five o'clock, threw a few things in the microwave, tossed a salad, and had dinner ready half an hour later.

I opened the refrigerator door and took out a custard all sprinkled with nutmeg. "Can I have this, Sophie?"

She nodded again without speaking. I sat down at the table opposite her. I had never known her to be so quiet. For once I wished she would say something. I spooned out the custard in neat little circles.

"Do you think those men will want to buy The Anchorage?" I finally asked.

Sophie didn't look up. "Could be."

"But if Great-Grandpa decides not to sell, it doesn't matter if they want to buy or not." It was becoming my theme song.

Sophie sliced off a carrot top. "There's ways."

My heart took a jump. "Like what?"

"Legal ways. Lester could be declared mentally unfit. That sort of thing. And it's true he's gone downhill bad since he broke his ankle last winter. Ayuh, there's ways."

"But Great-Grandpa's not mentally unfit. He's smarter than anyone." I shoved aside the empty custard cup. I felt sort of sick.

Sophie scooped up the carrots and dropped them in the pot. "You and me know that, but legal people is cleverer than you and me."

I didn't want to hear any more. I pushed back my chair, left the kitchen, and hurried through the dining room upstairs to my room. I fell on my bed, all hot and sweaty again. If only I could turn my brain to nonthink. I'd blast my thoughts out, that's what I'd do. I turned on my iPod and listened to my playlists at top volume until I had such a headache little hammers pounded inside my skull. It's not the noise, I told myself, it's the heat.

I opened the window wide and picked up *My Brother Sam Is Dead*. Summer reading list. Ugh. I flopped back on the bed and picked up where I'd left off. But I could feel myself drifting off to sleep and didn't fight it.

I was so groggy when I woke up, I must have been asleep for hours. At least Great-Grandpa must be awake by now. If his problems gave me a headache, think how awful he must feel. Yesterday he had enjoyed telling me about his sister Gwen's wedding in 1925. I'd try to find the photograph album for that year so we could look at the pictures together. I made my way down to the staircase landing.

But there were no 1925 albums in the secret panels. I looked through both sets of shelves. I found no albums dated after 1922 at all. I stared out the window trying to remember. The seals were basking on the rocks, but I hardly noticed them. Yes, I did remember. The first album I showed Great-Grandpa had been "Gwen, Louise, Fanny, Swanton Beach, Summer, 1924." Carefully, I checked all the shelves again. Every album after 1922 was gone, and no doubt about it.

Hmmm. The shelves were neat. Nothing was in disarray (a word Mom used to describe my bedroom). I wondered if anything else was missing. I took out all the black notebooks and piled them on the wide windowsill. They were still in order, beginning with the first year's book, 1882. But there wasn't a book in the pile beyond 1922. And yet . . . yet . . . I remembered reading Great-Great-Grandfather's diary for 1924, the year he almost lost his ship in a typhoon . . . or *was* it 1924?

The pattern for the letters was the same. They were all in order. And all neat. But there was not one single letter after 1922. I leaned my forehead against the cool window and shut my eyes. How long had everything been missing? That is, if they really *were* missing.

"*Humph,* you still rummaging around in those old things?"

I jumped a foot. Sophie's approach usually shook the floor, but I never heard her come up the stairs at all. My mouth went as dry as it does at the dentist's as Sophie stood looking over my shoulder at the letters and note-books lined up on the windowsill.

"They're interesting," was the bright remark I finally came up with.

Sophie humphed again and started up the second flight of stairs.

Our idiotic conversation must have got my brain going again. First, check with Great-Grandpa. I found him on the Bridge watching the seals through his telescope.

"Do you know when your father stopped writing let-ters home?" I asked.

"When he retired from the sea, of course." Great-Grandpa looked at me as if I were stupid. "Nineteen two five, that's when. Same year he stopped keeping his logs."

"Do you have some of the letters and albums here on the Bridge or in your room?"

"Nope, I've counted on you to put everything away," he answered.

Okay, now to launch Plan Two. Mom just might have taken the books to her room to read at night. She said without a cigarette, it was hard to fall asleep. And I knew she had The Anchorage blueprints on her closet shelf. When Mom decorates a house, she always has the blue-prints photographed, reduced in size, and framed as a housewarming present. She had already taken The Anchorage blueprints so that when we went back to New York, she could have them made up and framed as a surprise for Great-Grandpa.

With a quick "I'll be back" I left the Bridge, and ran through the living room and up the stairs to Mom's room. In just the time we'd been in The Anchorage, it already looked like a Margaret Lauder Room. She had brought in some plants, and found an old afghan and thrown it over her bed. She had taken down the old curtains and stitched up new ones out of flowered sheets. What I liked best was it smelled of cologne and hair spray and not stale cigarette smoke. I thought of poor Mom's next two days with Harvey and Mrs. La Bronquist. Hang in there, Mom, and DON'T SMOKE. I sent mental brain waves.

The blueprints were still on her closet shelf, but the books and letters and albums weren't anywhere in the room. It didn't surprise me. If Mom had been reading them, I was sure she'd have returned them before leaving the island. I was stumped. Slowly, I went back down the stairs to put everything else away in the panels. I had just climbed up on the windowsill when I heard Bert Smith's bell. Three times. Then more. Five, six, seven. On and on it rang. Maybe it wasn't Bert at all. Maybe it was someone being funny.

Above me a door slammed and footsteps ran down the hall. Sophie appeared at the head of the stairs. She grabbed the banister, and down she came, her oxfords hitting each step with a thud.

"What is it?" I shouted as she pounded past me.

"Bert Smith. Something's happened."

I took the stairs two at a time after her. "What do you mean?"

"Last time Bert come out like that, my daughter's farmhouse had burned to the ground." By now Sophie was on her way out the front door with me right behind her. When she reached the cliff stairs, she was so winded she had to stop. I stopped, too.

"You mean there's been an accident or something?" My voice squeaked. All I could think of was Mom and what had happened to her parents. It was as if someone had grabbed me around the ribs and squeezed. I could hardly breathe.

"Bert wouldn't give us a fright like that 'less it was important," Sophie started down the cliff stairs.

Bert's bell echoed in my head as if it were a million miles away, and my knees went so weak I could hardly stand. I braced myself on the railing as everything blurred in front of me.

THIRTEEN

Two Alone

I closed my eyes until everything steadied. When I opened them, Sophie was halfway down the stairs. I took off after her.

"—don't want to take no chances. It means X-rays and whatnot," Bert was saying to Sophie when I reached them.

I grabbed Sophie's arm. "What happened?"

"My sister Esther was in an auto accident. She run up against a tree, and they took her to the hospital over in Swanton." Sophie held her hand over her heart as if to still its beating.

"That's terrible," I managed to say. And I meant it. But such a relief flooded over me I felt dizzy again.

"Bert don't think she's too bad. But she's alone. I'm all the family she's got." Sophie's booming voice wavered.

"I figgered you'd want to go straight to the hospital, so Roger and me come out 'stead of radioing the news." Bert took off his cap and ran his fingers through his thin hair. "We'll wait whilst you get your things together."

Sophie looked at me. "But what about Lester and Kimball? It don't seem right to leave 'em."

I was so relieved about Mom, anything was okay. Don't worry about Great-Grandpa and me. We'll be fine."

Still, Sophie hesitated. "You don't think your ma would mind?"

"I'm sure she'd say to go," I insisted.

Sophie started back up the stairs. It was as if she had used up all her energy getting down. Now she leaned on the guardrail and took each step slowly.

Bert reboarded the *Lucky Sue* and pulled out a newspaper to pass the time. Roger sat at the end of the dock. He'd taken off his sneakers and dangled his feet in the water. I sat down beside him.

"Whew, some hot day." He waved his cap like a fan.

I took off my sneakers and stuck my feet in the water, too. Wow, it was cold! There must be an inverse theory. The hotter the air, the colder the water. "Was Esther Goff hurt bad?"

"I dunno anything about it. Bert just told me we had to come out here for Sophie," Roger answered. "You drove up with Esther from Portland. You oughtta know what a lousy driver she is."

I sure did. I glanced back to see if Bert could hear us. "Tell me what Bert and Sophie are like," I asked in a low voice.

Roger looked up, surprised. "That's a funny question. They're old pals, I guess. They're always talking and whispering around. And Bert sure comes out here to Shag more'n any of the other islands. 'Course I never worked for Bert before this summer. He's real quiet and sorta grumpy. We don't talk much at all."

Roger pulled out a pack of gum, took a piece, and offered one to me. This time the peppermint smell got to me, and I knew how Mom must feel about smoking. Braces or not, I couldn't resist.

"Are you going to stay in Watoset all your life, Roger, where you know everybody and everybody knows you?" The gum tasted really good as I worked it into a chewable coil in my mouth.

"I *am* not! Soon's I can, I'm heading west to live in the wild like a mountain man."

That was a new one to me. "What's a mountain man?"

"Are you kidding? You don't know?" Roger snorted. "Mountain men like Jim Bridger and Joe Meek and Jedediah Smith explored the West more than a hundred years ago. They lived in the wilderness and trapped beaver and wrestled bears with only a knife. . . ."

It was like turning on a talking encyclopedia. I never heard so much information on something I knew nothing about. It was the first time Roger had ever mentioned how crazy he was to go west. I was so intent on what he had to say I didn't notice Sophie come back down the cliff stairs until she was on the dock. She carried a little plastic suitcase like the one that came with my old Barbie doll.

"Now, Kimball, I spoke to Lester, and everything's set. The stew for supper is all done. Lester can make his own breakfast coffee, and there's blueberry muffins—"

"C'mon, gal. I thought you was in a hurry," Bert shouted from the *Lucky Sue*. He had already started up the motor.

"I'll bring out my Jim Bridger biography next trip," Roger called over his shoulder as he jumped aboard.

His offer really pleased me. The proud way he said it, I knew it was his best book.

"I'll be back tomorrow, sure," Sophie yelled from the boat. "If I'm not here by noon, warm up that half a chicken from yesterday and . . ." Sophie's instructions were drowned out by the motor as Bert pulled away from the dock. She cupped her mouth with her hands, and I could see she was still shouting, but I couldn't hear her. Bliss. I waved good-bye.

As the *Lucky Sue*'s motor faded away and the little waves from her wake stopped rippling against the dock, it was suddenly very quiet. Then it hit me. Great-Grandpa and I were alone on Shag Island. No Mom. No Sophie. Just Great-Grandpa and me. And Dash. Not exactly Lassie the Wonder Dog. Was Great-Grandpa babysitting for me or was I sitting for him?

"Ho, there!"

It was Great-Grandpa at the top of the cliff stairs signaling to me. With the huge house outlined behind him and the lowering sun throwing his bent figure into shadows, I knew who was in charge. Me. After all, I was twelve and he was ninety-three. I was three inches taller and stronger by far. Somehow, realizing he had to count on me made me feel better than if I were counting on him.

"It was lucky Esther Goff wasn't hurt bad," Great-Grandpa commented when I reached him. "That Esther's independent as a hog on ice. She'll send Sophie back straightaway, wait and see."

I laughed. In a way it was nice to have Sophie gone. Without her constant chatter, our meals would be peaceful. And those missing books and letters made me uneasy. Not that I was sure any were even missing, but with Sophie gone, I could really search the house for them. Even, it crossed my mind, in Sophie's room.

Supper wasn't so hot. I had never cooked on a woodstove, and I scorched the stew. Great-Grandpa said it was fine, but it wasn't, and neither of us ate much. After supper, we sat on the Bridge and watched the sun set in a weird yellowish sky.

"Have you ever heard of mountain men?" I asked Great-Grandpa.

"Ayuh," he answered right away. "Mountain men opened the West. Like sailors going into uncharted seas, mountain men went into the uncharted West.

"The West . . ." Great-Grandpa chuckled his nice chuckle. "When I was about ten, Mother and I went west by train. Father hadn't been home in over two years, so

Mother left Gwen and Warren behind and took me with her, me being the most obstreperous of the three children. Mother and I sailed on Father's ship for three months up and down the West Coast from San Francisco to Vancouver, British Columbia, and back again. It was quite an adventure."

Great-Grandpa's expression changed. He looked sad. "The West is different now, like everything else. Ayuh, in my lifetime, I've gone from horse and buggies to astronauts blasting off into space. You know, a man can live too long . . . like Father. I don't want my mind to go like that. Sometimes I feel it happening to me. . . ."

"Oh, no, that's not true!" I fast tried to think of something to change the subject. "How about some dominoes?"

But Great-Grandpa wouldn't be distracted. "I can't leave The Anchorage. Once out, it'd be easy to have me put away. Like Father, I'd end up on the poor farm."

"But there's no such thing anymore." I was beginning to panic.

"It wasn't called the poor farm when Father went there, either. It had a fancy name like Cozy Acres. Still and all, it was the poor farm," Great-Grandpa insisted. "And sometimes I feel my mind is slipping, too. I'm afraid. There's ways lawyers got. No, I got to stay on here at The Anchorage."

"There's ways." It's just what Sophie had said. "But, Great-Grandpa, you have Social Security and . . ." I tried to remember what else Mom had told me. "You can buy a house in Watoset, and we'll come visit you every summer."

Great-Grandpa reached for his cane and stood up. "Weather's coming in with the next shift of the tide. I'm going to bed."

I jumped up, too. I'd really bombed out. Now Great-Grandpa was all upset. I followed him into the living room. Dash was waiting by the door. After the flat yellow light of the Bridge, I stumbled in the sudden shadowed darkness of the living room.

"Maybe we could leave some lights on," I hinted.

"Nonsense. Waste of electricity," Great-Grandpa snapped.

So we picked our way through the dark living room with Dash right between us. The antlers on the walls threw spiked shadows like bare tree branches reaching out to grab us. As I followed Great-Grandpa's slow progress up the stairs, I only glanced at the stacks of books and letters on the window ledge. I'd put them away tomorrow, for sure.

We made our unlit way through the dark halls. My bedroom door was closed. Had I left it that way? I couldn't remember.

"Will you wait while I check my room, Great-Grandpa?" I asked.

He looked at me as if he couldn't remember who I was. His eyes were focused in a funny vacant stare. Before he could change his mind, I opened my door and quick flicked on all the lights. The heck with the electricity. I searched in the closet, under the bed, behind the chairs. Just as I turned on the bathroom light, I heard Great-Grandpa open his bedroom door across from mine, then shut it. He must have forgotten all about me. That was okay. I was set for the night. I had already taken off my sneakers when I heard a hoarse shout from next door.

"Help! Stop! Go away. . . ." There was a smashing and banging from Great-Grandpa's room. I ran out into the hall. Dash stood in front of Great-Grandpa's closed door, whimpering. From inside, I heard Great-Grandpa yell again.

"Oh, no, look out!"

There was a wild screech, then another crash. Silence. I turned the doorknob with a shaky hand, afraid to go in, but even more afraid not to.

FOURTEEN

A Ghostly
Performance

Would Great-Grandpa's room be dark? I said a quick prayer and opened the door. A glow of light greeted me. But it shone on Great-Grandpa slumped against his bed. His eyes were open, but he stared past me unseeing. Dash rushed into the room. Whining, he nuzzled his face up against Great-Grandpa.

I bent over Great-Grandpa, too. "What happen—"

Swoosh. Something sailed over my head with a shriek. I screamed and dropped on my hands and knees to the floor.

"Oh, no!" Great-Grandpa cried out.

With my head scrunched between my shoulders, I peeked up at the far side of the room. There, perched on the stop of a bookcase, was a bird. Not just-any-old-bird, but a strange-looking bird with a yellow face and long tail feathers. He was like a parrot, only gray, not green.

He opened his curved beak. YA-AAK.

I was so unstrung, I wasn't sure if the squawk had come

from me or the bird. Dash was unstrung, too. He cocked his head to one side and whimpered. The bird stretched and fluttered his wings. I ducked, sure he would come zooming across the room again. But nothing happened. When I looked up, the bird was staring at us, his shiny black eyes blinking.

"One of Father's birds . . ." Great-Grandpa whispered.

A shiver went through me. The funny bird *did* look like the birds in the old photograph albums. I studied the bird while he studied us. The only birds I'd seen like that were in the Bronx Zoo World of Birds. My heart picked up a thumping rhythm. How had he ever gotten in here?

"It's just a bird." Which was no help at all. But it was the best I could do.

Great-Grandpa's salt-and-pepper eyebrows stamped dark lines in his pale face. "I came in my room . . . shut the door. When I turned on the light, I fancied I saw a bird on my bedpost. It was the kind Father used to bring home . . . the bird seemed so real I tried to chase him out with my cane. I broke a lamp . . . and the mirror."

Great-Grandpa thought the bird was in his imagination!

"But the bird is right over there on your bookcase. See." But Great-Grandpa's head was sunk on his chest. He wouldn't look up.

"Ever since you and Margaret came, I haven't heard the Chinese music or seen the lighthouse lights. I never said a thing to Sophie about the music or the lights." Great-Grandpa's voice was so low it was hard to hear him. I bent closer. "I thought I was better. Now with this . . . this . . .

bird, it's like I feared. When Father's mind went, he heard Chinese music and saw lighthouse lights. And Chinese junks on the bay. I'm losing my mind just like him."

"No, you're not!"

My cry startled the bird. He squawked again and flapped his wings. Dash barked. That finished the bird. He took off from his perch and swooped low over our heads out the open door. Fearless now, Dash barked and barked. With the bird gone, I felt braver, too. I got up off my hands and knees and quick shut the door. Then I tugged at Great-Grandpa to get him on the bed.

"Listen to me." I spoke distinctly. "There was a bird here. I saw him. He was a gray parroty bird with a yellow face, and he just flew out the door."

"Father loved to bring home tropical birds. Sometimes Fanny Tillis could get them to talk. . . ."

He wasn't registering. I had to get through to him. "I heard that Chinese music the same as you. The very first night I was here I heard it plain as anything."

It worked. For the first time he looked at me. The glazed expression left his eyes and he focused on my face. "You heard Chinese music?"

"The night we arrived."

His face brightened, then clouded over. "You're a Kimball. Madness is in the blood."

Madness is right. But not the kind Great-Grandpa meant. I stamped my foot. "Darn it, I'm a Lauder, too, and have plenty of their blood. I heard the music and saw the bird as plain as I see Dash right now."

"Then where is he?"

"I told you he just flew out the door. He's somewhere in the house." Or better yet, out an open window, I added under my breath.

"I know you only want to help, but I don't care to discuss it further. I'm going to bed. Let Dash out, please." Great-Grandpa limped his way across the room and bent down for his cane. The floor was covered with slivers of broken mirror. "Good night," he said with dignity.

That seemed to be that. I called Dash, who followed me out into the hall. As he settled in a boneless heap on his little rug, I remembered the bird. I like birds. I had a canary for two years. But he was tame. And smaller. I stuck my head around the corner of my room.

"Fly away. Go home."

There was no answering screech or beating of wings. I tiptoed back into my room and checked everywhere. Once I was sure he wasn't around, I turned on my iPod. Then I jumped into bed, still dressed. Sleep was about as far away as Mom in New York. I just lay listening to the music and thinking . . . thinking. . . .

First I had to convince Great-Grandpa that he hadn't imagined the bird. And that he wasn't going crazy like his father. Then I would have to figure out some way to get the bird out of the house. What worried me more was how he had gotten in. Great-Grandpa's windows had been shut. And that was no little local bird that might have flown down a chimney.

I sat up straight. This morning, when Mr. Tate and his

clients had come out to The Anchorage in the *Lucky Sue,* Bert had handed Sophie a big picnic basket. The bird must have been inside. It would have been easy enough for Sophie to put the bird in Great-Grandpa's room before she left for the mainland.

Sophie. Her face kept coming back to me. Even Roger said she and Bert were always whispering. Or was it plotting? She had been awfully uptight about my finding the letters and books. And why was she so frantic to get the mail before Great-Grandpa? As for her sister, maybe she hadn't even had an accident. Roger hadn't heard anything about it. Sophie and Bert might have cooked up the story just to get Great-Grandpa and me alone on Shag Island. And Bert knew all about radios. He could have piped in the Chinese music somehow.

Chinkley-chime-chime. My eyes flew open. I must have fallen asleep thinking about the Chinese music. But I was awake. And I could hear the music coming from some distant place. I jumped out of bed and was in the hall before I had time to think. Dash was still curled into a furry pretzel outside Great-Grandpa's half-open door.

"Great-Grandpa, do you hear that music?"

There was no answer. I pushed the door open the rest of the way and the music was suddenly louder. And the room was ablaze with light. Great-Grandpa was sitting up in bed, his eyes wide. A sound rattled in his throat, but no words came out. Without warning, the room went black. The tinkly chimes, even eerier in the darkness, filled the room without seeming to come from any one direction.

"Turn on a light!" I yelled.

There was no response from Great-Grandpa. Just as I started to feel my way toward his bed, the room was flooded with the same blinding light as before. Trapped in the beam, I threw myself next to Great-Grandpa on the bed. The light swept across the room, then went off, leaving us in darkness.

"It's the pirate lighthouse." Great-Grandpa's voice came out of the night like a pronouncement from above.

I struggled not to scream. "Turn on your light," I hissed through clenched teeth.

Miracle of miracles, this time, Great-Grandpa must have heard me. There was a click as he turned on his bedside lamp.

Then flash. The bright glare of light filled the room again as the music tinkled on.

"That pirate lighthouse beam beckoned Father's ship up on the rocks off Hainan. Now the lighthouse is beckoning me." Great-Grandpa was talking to himself. I don't think he even knew I was there.

The light *was* like a lighthouse beam flashing on and off. But I knew there was no lighthouse outside. It must have been rigged up somehow. Maybe it was Bert, shining the *Lucky Sue*'s light into Great-Grandpa's window.

"Listen," I said. "Someone's trying to scare you into thinking you're crazy. But you're not! I see those lights. And hear that music, too."

Wait, I could tape the music. Then Great-Grandpa would know it wasn't all in his head. But that meant leaving the safety of his bed. Move, Kimball, I ordered. I watched my feet swing off the bed, just as the dazzling light blacked out. I took a deep breath, raced out the door and across the hall to my room, snatched up my radio and a new tape, sped back to Great-Grandpa's room, jumped on his bed, and let out my breath like I had swum the distance underwater. Dash sauntered in behind me. My hands shook as I took out the family history tape that Great-Grandpa and I had been recording and slipped in the new tape.

"What are you doing?" Great-Grandpa asked dully as the room was flooded with a blaze of light. It was like being photographed under a hundred spotlights.

"I'm going to tape the music."

The music played on and then, as abruptly as they had begun, the music and the lights switched off. The only sound in the room was Dash's wheezing.

"It's o . . . o . . . over," I stuttered.

I looked at Great-Grandpa. He sat as before, one hand gripping the bedpost, the other his blanket. His vacant eyes stared. Maybe he *was* crazy. All of a sudden tears filled my eyes and trickled down my cheeks. I fell back against the headboard and sobbed and sobbed. I couldn't stop. We might be killed, and no one would know. Mom would come back and find us dead. I didn't even have the strength to wipe my nose.

FIFTEEN

Discovery in a Desk

When I woke up, I was still on Great-Grandpa's bed and stiff all over. I wiggled my shoulders to get the kinks out. What a night. Nightmare was more like it. At least we were still alive. I was, anyway. But Great-Grandpa was gone. I slid off the bed and just missed stepping on my glasses. They must have fallen to the floor in the night. I put them on and looked at the clock. Only six thirty. But it was such a dreary morning it might as well have been midnight. Rain beat against the closed windows.

"Great-Grandpa, where are you?"

Above the sound of the rain, I heard water running. The bathroom door opened, and Great-Grandpa came out. He looked the same as he had my first morning on Shag Island. That is, terrible. He was pale and had dark circles under his eyes. He shuffled over to the window and stared out at the slashing rain. Dash padded after him.

"Great-Grandpa, what are we going to do about the bird?"

Great-Grandpa turned around and shook his finger at me. "There was no bird." His voice was stern.

No bird? "But I was right here. I saw the bird and the flashing lights. And heard the Chinese music, too. So did Dash. He barked his head off."

We both looked down at Dash. He had slumped to the floor with his head collapsed on his paws. Had Dash really been barking his head off? It didn't seem possible.

Great-Grandpa thumped his cane on the floor with a trace of his old spark. "It's over and done with. No more talk about it or they'll be saying I'm daft."

"But you're not daft. And I can prove it. Remember how I recorded that music last night? It's all right here on my tape." Then again, maybe it wasn't. Maybe Great-Grandpa was right. Maybe we were both crazy. No, I *had* heard the music. I rewound the tape, then pressed the Play button.

And out it came, the same Chinese music. It wasn't very clear, but clear enough. Plenty clear enough. Great-Grandpa moved closer, but he didn't say a word. The music ended, and my voice came on. "It's o . . . o . . . over." Then there was the sound of my crying.

Embarrassed, I turned the radio off. "That's it."

Great-Grandpa just stood there. Then he leaned down and rubbed Dash behind the ears. "Can you play it again?"

I rewound the tape and played it over.

Great-Grandpa was silent, his eyebrows in a thinking frown. "You could play that as many times as you want?"

I nodded. "A thousand times."

There was another pregnant pause. I wasn't sure what a "pregnant pause" was, but I'd heard the expression often enough to know that it described Great-Grandpa's silence. He fingered his mustache. "But if the music was real, and the lights and the bird, too, what put them all in motion?"

At last he believed me. Now we could do something. Like call the police. Or get off Shag Island. "Someone must have played that music over a radio. Or on an iPod docked into a speaker. How long have you heard the music? Did you hear it the night Mom and I arrived?"

"Let's see . . . ayuh, that must have been the last time. But it's been going on since last winter when I got back from the hospital. I'm always asleep . . . the music and the lights wake me. I never told a soul, not even Sophie. If anyone knew, they'd say my mind was going like Father's. They'd try to put me away like him. . . ." Great-Grandpa's voice trailed off. Then he cleared his throat and went on. "That bird last night was just like the birds Father used to bring home. How did he get in?"

"Sophie must have done it." I went over everything I had figured out the night before. Bert and Sophie in cahoots. Sophie having a fit at my discovery of the secret panels. The possibility her sister hadn't even had an accident.

Great-Grandpa humphed. "Sophie? That's ridiculous. Why, when her husband, Frank, died, I took her in, gave her a job and a place to live. Sophie would never do that to me."

"I bet anything those missing diaries and albums are in her room." As soon as I said it, I knew I was right. In the back of my mind, I was sure all along that's where they were. "Come with me, and I'll prove it to you."

Great-Grandpa shook his head. "I'd never go in Sophie's room without her being here."

I groaned. Great-Grandpa was most certainly Kimball-stubborn. He made everything an uphill battle. "Then I'll go to Sophie's room and look myself," I announced.

"It's not right," Great-Grandpa said, halfheartedly. Just to test him, I started for the door. If he tried to stop me, I wouldn't go.

But he didn't. "Dash and I'll go down and commence breakfast," he said instead.

Okay, that settled it. I'd go. I headed down the hall. The overcast sky made the house as dismal as a dungeon. I turned on every light I passed. But the bulbs couldn't have been more than twenty-five watts. All they did was throw scary shadows on the walls. I walked faster and faster. That bird was still loose. Somewhere. I turned right at the end of the hall and scooted toward Sophie's room.

I cracked open the door, not sure I had the right room. But I did. Besides a flowered rug on the floor and a green plaid bedspread and matching curtains that screamed "Sophie," her old sewing machine was on the table. I headed for her rolltop desk and reached for the lid. I hesitated. Somehow, I couldn't open it. Being a private investigator wasn't as easy as TV shows made it look.

Ahem. Someone cleared his throat behind me. Sophie

was back. My heart took off like Dad's new Porsche. I spun around. It was only Great-Grandpa, looking sheepish.

"It's not your responsibility to do this. I either got to fish or cut bait." He limped across the room with Dash right behind him. We stood together staring at the closed desk for a minute, listening to the pepper of rain against the windows and the trickle of water running down a gutter.

"I came 'cause you got me to thinking," Great-Grandpa finally said. "Sophie *has* been acting peculiar of late. Secretivelike. She's been using the radio, too, when she thought I was napping, though she claims she doesn't know how to work it. Still and all, I can't abide meddling."

He just couldn't bring himself to open the desk either. But someone had to do it. I reached down and slid back the top. The desk was as neat as the rest of the room, and right away we could see there was nothing interesting on it. After only a second's hesitation Great-Grandpa sat down in the desk chair and pulled open the top drawer. It was full of writing paper and old boxed Christmas cards and used wrapping paper.

"See, what'd I tell you? There's nothing here." Great-Grandpa sounded relieved. He opened the second drawer. It was arranged with pads of yellow-lined paper and bills and letters all clipped together. It certainly wasn't the old diaries and letters we were looking for. But Great-Grandpa gasped. Then he reached in and took everything out. He spread the yellow sheets and letters on the desk.

"I swear." He breathed out the words. His brown spotted hands trembled as he took his glasses out from his cardigan pocket and put them on. He looked through everything carefully.

"What is it, Great-Grandpa?"

He pounded his fist on the desk. "I don't believe it!"

I leaned over the desk to see better. There were bills and letters, all addressed to Mr. Lester A. Kimball. And the yellow-lined sheets were covered with cursive, the same heavy handwriting I remembered from Great-Grandpa's letter to Mom and me. Other sheets were nothing but a signature over and over. "Lester A. Kimball." "Lester A. Kimball."

I was really puzzled. "I don't understand."

Great-Grandpa's pale-blue eyes seemed to shoot sparks. "It's mail addressed to me. But I never saw any of it. And this is my signature that Sophie has been practicing. She must have sent letters out in my name. Look at this." Great-Grandpa slapped a letter in my hand. It was from Merritt, Parsons, Inc., Boston, Mass.

> Dear Mr. Kimball,
> Enclosed is our check in the amount of $1,500 to cover your shipment of July 12th. We would be happy to hear from you again in regard to the purchase of anything more from your fine collection. Thank you for considering our services.
>
> Sincerely yours,
> John P. Crowell

Fifteen hundred dollars! The amount rocked me back

on my heels. "Did you ever get the money?" I asked.

Great-Grandpa shook his head. "Never. Sophie must have forged my name to the check and cashed it." All of a sudden the anger went out of him. I could almost see him physically deflate. He picked up a pad of yellow paper. It was covered with his signature, lines and lines of it. Then he dropped it on the desk and took off his glasses. "To think that Sophie would do something like this." He stood up and walked over to the window. He stared out at the rain weeping down the pane.

Then it hit me. Of course that was what had happened to Mom's and my invitation to Shag Island. "Remember how surprised you were when Mom and I arrived, Great-Grandpa? It must have been Sophie who wrote to us in your handwriting. Then, when Mom wrote back accepting the invitation, Sophie made sure you never saw the letter. So you didn't forget we were coming. You never knew. And that's why Sophie wants to get the mail first. She must be opening all your letters."

"Could be . . . could be . . . but something doesn't make sense." Great-Grandpa tapped his finger on the windowpane. "If it was Sophie and Bert who rigged everything up to frighten me, like you say, then why would Sophie write and ask you and your mother to come visit? 'Pears to me, Bert and Sophie were in the catbird seat, especially with money like this coming in. They wouldn't dare risk everything by having you and Margaret up here poking around."

Great-Grandpa just had to be sharper than anyone I

knew. Here I thought I was such a genius to figure everything out. But he was right. There was no reason Sophie and Bert would want Mom and me on Shag Island. The puzzle didn't fit together as neatly as I had thought.

SIXTEEN

Confiding in Roger

Great-Grandpa turned from the window and walked back to Sophie's desk. He began to straighten it up. "I won't pry anymore. Sophie and I will have it out soon as she gets back today."

That was the last thing I expected. "But . . . but I thought we might make up some excuse to ride back to Watoset with Bert. Then we could go straight to the police."

Great-Grandpa scowled. "I told you before, nothing is going to get me out of The Anchorage. No, I'll set down with Sophie and thrash out this whole business."

Scritchh . . . Scritchh . . . A sound like fingernails scraping on the window scared the next words right out of me. I spun around. It was only the wind tapping a broken branch against the house.

"You're jumpier than a mess of herring in a barrel," Great-Grandpa grumbled. "Why don't *you* go back with Bert and wait for your ma in town?"

That sounded even worse. I couldn't act normal for five minutes with Bert, let alone for that long boat trip. Besides, I had made up my mind yesterday, hadn't I, that I was going to watch out for Great-Grandpa?

"I'd rather stay. Still, there must be something we can do. Like radio the police."

"Forget the police. Why, if I told them music plays out here at night, and lights flash on and off, they'd say I was crazy as a coot." Great-Grandpa banged the desk top down. "I want my coffee and something to eat. Right now."

Dash led the way downstairs, sort of thumping down two legs at a time. I wondered at what age a dog stopped running downstairs and started easing down them like Dash. When he reached the bottom, he stopped short and growled. It wasn't a ferocious growl. It was more a "Oh-no-not-you-again" growl. Great-Grandpa and I stopped too. We both looked up.

There was the bird sitting on a big rack of deer antlers that hung by the front door as if it were his private perch. He stretched his wings deliberately, then flapped them hard and hopped up to the next point of the antlers. It wasn't as if he didn't know we were there. I was sure he did. He was just putting on a little act for us.

I giggled. What had been so terrifying in the night was irresistible in the morning. Great-Grandpa must have thought so, too.

"I guess no one told Jack Parrot he was supposed to be a figment of my imagination," he chuckled. His laugh sounded so great and I was so glad he could joke about what had happened, I wanted to hug him. Instead, I slipped my hand in his, and we held hands all the way to the kitchen.

"One time Father brought back a handsome parrot from Brazil. Sailors on shipboard were called Jack, so that's what we named the bird," Great-Grandpa explained as he started up the fire in the woodstove. "We had Jack for over ten years, and though he was bigger than this bird, he had the same smart look. My, parrots are clever. Fanny Tillis got Jack to do simple tricks. And talk, too."

"Can we catch this Jack Parrot?" I asked.

"Most parrots are pretty friendly, and if they've been in captivity at all, they're apt to be some tamed," Great-Grandpa said. "After breakfast, you might give it a try."

When I'd stuffed myself with orange juice, a blueberry muffin, apple pie, and hot chocolate, I found a crab net. And a broom for good measure. But Great-Grandpa kept eating and pouring himself more coffee. How could such a small man eat so much? And so slowly. We had a lot to do before Bert brought Sophie back. First of all, I wanted to find where that music had been coming from. Then we had to look for something to put Jack Parrot in. After that, we had to catch Jack.

"I'll wash the dishes later." I grabbed Great-Grandpa's finally empty plates and ran toward the sink with them.

"Careful. That's the china Father brought back from Shanghai," Great-Grandpa said. "Say, do you s'pose Sophie could be selling Father's china to that firm in Boston? I can't think of anything else of value 'round here."

He limped over to the china cupboard and looked inside. "One, two, three, four . . ." He counted every dish, cup, and saucer. "Nope, they're all here. What *is* Sophie selling?"

I shrugged. "I don't know. The house is full of stuff." As I spoke, Great-Grandpa took a toothpick from a box on the windowsill and began to clean his teeth. Carefully. I could have groaned. Getting Great-Grandpa to hurry was like running up a down escalator. I looked out the kitchen window. It was raining as hard as ever. Or harder. Wisps of damp cold and fog crept into the house. I shivered and rubbed my arms, wishing I had put on a sweater.

"Now we can play dominoes till Bert brings Sophie back," Great-Grandpa said. "It's a good game for a squally day."

"But I thought we could look for where that music was coming from last night," I protested. "Then catch Jack Parrot—"

"Not me," Great-Grandpa interrupted. "I got a breakfast to digest, and settin' is the best way to do it."

With my crab net and broom, I followed Great-Grandpa into the hall. But Jack Parrot was gone. I might as well forget him for now. A wily bird like that could be anywhere. I debated whether to go upstairs alone to look for where the music had been set up. The wide staircase was dark, and the rain threw itself against the landing windows as if in a rage to get in. I'll go up later, I decided.

After I digest my breakfast. For now, being with Great-Grandpa suited me fine.

But I couldn't keep my mind on dominoes. It was as if someone else were playing and I was watching. Great-Grandpa beat me easily, game after game. The rain and wind slammed against the Bridge windows. The spruce trees snapped first in one direction, then in another. Whitecaps iced every wave. I have no idea how long we played. It seemed like forever.

"Bert's bell," Great-Grandpa announced abruptly. He stood up.

I hadn't even heard it. That meant Sophie was back. I didn't want to face her. My expression was sure to give me away. But I couldn't resist following Great-Grandpa through the living room and into the hall. He opened the front door. There was a sharp bang-bang-bang from outside.

It startled me. "What's that?"

"It must be the dining-room shutter," Great-Grandpa said. "A good wind always shakes it loose."

From the front porch we couldn't see the dock. So we just had to wait for Sophie to climb the cliff stairs. I was so tense the steady pounding of the shutter set my teeth in their tight braces to aching.

Suddenly two figures in rain slickers appeared, trudging up the steps. Right away I saw the first one was Bert, skinny as a flagpole and just as straight. But the second one wasn't as big as Sophie. It *wasn't* Sophie. It was Roger.

I stood as close to the edge of the porch as I could without getting drenched. But even on tiptoe, I didn't see Sophie. She wasn't with them.

Bert and Roger crossed the yard toward us. Roger was barefoot and carrying a cooler. Though I was relieved not to see Sophie, in a way I was disappointed. In the back of my mind I guess I wanted Great-Grandpa to have it out with her, and be done with it, too. Cliff-hanging, to stretch a pun, wasn't my bag.

"Where's Sophie?" Great-Grandpa called over the wind.

"She figgered she'd better stay another day," Bert answered as he and Roger reached us. "Esther's gonna be awright, but she needs more tests. Sophie made me promise to check on you two and bring out your mail and paper. And she sent more eats in the cooler. You know Sophie. She ain't happy 'less she's fussing about food."

Great-Grandpa was fantastic. He was strictly poker-faced. "I don't know what I'd do without Sophie." He opened the front door. "C'mon in. You both look like you could use a cup of hot coffee. Say, Roger, fix that dining-room shutter before you head back, will you? I'd 'preciate it."

"Sure." Roger agreed. And we all went in the house.

"I saw Doug Tate this morning," Bert said. He and Roger took off their slickers and shook them. A shower of water sprinkled on the hall rug. "Those men that came out were real pleased with The Anchorage. Mebbe if they saw it today, they'd feel different."

"Ayuh, a sou'wester's pretty gloomy." Great-Grandpa gave a short laugh. Still talking, he and Bert disappeared into the dining room.

"I brought you my Jim Bridger biography," Roger said. He took the lid off the cooler and pulled out a book wrapped in plastic.

As I took the book, my determination caved in. I just had to tell someone what was going on, and Roger was the only person I could trust. Besides, Bert's mention of Doug Tate had given me an idea. I took Roger's arm and led him to the staircase. He gave me a funny look as I sat down and pulled him down beside me.

"I've got to talk to you," I blurted out.

And talk I did. About everything. The bird, the music, the lights, the missing letters and notebooks, and Sophie's forgeries. Roger never said a word. He just stared at me with a surprised look that made his freckles stand out like uneven polka dots.

"So what I decided was this." I was almost out of breath, but the last part was the most important. "As soon as you get to Watoset, call Mr. Tate and ask him to come out here. Don't tell him what I told you, or he might go to the police and Great-Grandpa would be furious. Just say we're in trouble and need help. And make sure you don't say anything to Bert or Sophie."

Roger stared at me as if I had freaked out. "Wow, are you crazy? Old Bert Smith and Sophie Cluett a big crime syndicate?" He shook his head a couple of times. "You must have heard that music on Sophie's old radio. And seen lights coming in from some ship. And that bird coulda gotten in the house any time. Or maybe you were just dreaming it all."

"That's dumb. Great-Grandpa and I wouldn't have the same dream."

Roger stood up. "I'd better fix that shutter. We have the other islands to cover, and Bert'll want to be getting back." He shook his head again as he started for the kitchen.

I just sat on the stairs after Roger left, close to tears. I was so sure he would help us. But he didn't believe me. Now I'd gone and blown everything. Why, he'd probably run and tell Bert the whole story. And wouldn't that just dump Great-Grandpa and me out of the frying pan and into the fire.

SEVENTEEN

A Welcome Visitor

Bert was anxious to push off, so after Roger repaired the shutter, the two of them left in the *Lucky Sue*. Roger avoided speaking to me again. Or even looking at me. I felt both furious that he didn't believe me and worried that he would tell Bert everything. I just had to do something to keep my mind off *that* possibility.

"Breakfast must be digested by now. How about trying to find where that music came from last night?" I asked Great-Grandpa as we closed the door on Bert and Roger. I couldn't face any more dominoes.

Great-Grandpa looked grumpy. "All right, but to tell the truth, now I know the music isn't in my mind, I don't much care where it was coming from. Once we hear it again, we can track it down. Right now, I'd sooner read my paper."

Well, I cared. I wasn't interested in hearing that music

again. Not ever. I waited while Great-Grandpa put his mail and the paper on the hall table. Then we headed upstairs with Dash tagging along behind us.

"This is like looking for a needle in a haystack. Where in tarnation are you going to commence?" Great-Grandpa demanded as we stood in the middle of his bedroom.

"First I'd better clean up the broken mirror." I'd forgotten all about it. And the broken lamp. After I'd thrown all the pieces of glass and china in the wastebasket, I began my search. I checked in the closet, the bathroom, under the bed, behind the pictures on the walls, beneath the bookcase, even in the bureau drawers. Nothing. At least nothing turned up that might have played that awful music. Of course, it could have come from a peanut-size-James-Bond gadget, but somehow, I doubted it. Great-Grandpa was growing more and more impatient.

"Are you satisfied?" he asked after I'd poked my head in the fireplace and looked up the chimney.

"Just because I can't find it for now doesn't mean I'm going to give up."

"Well, I am. You can stay here and do what you want, but I'm itching to get my hands on that newspaper and see what the Red Sox are up to." Great-Grandpa started for the door.

I hated to admit defeat, but I didn't feel like poking around by myself. So without an argument, I followed Great-Grandpa back down the stairs. As we passed the landing, I glanced at the notebooks and letters on the window ledge that I still hadn't straightened up from yesterday. "You go ahead. I'm going to put these things away," I said.

As I sorted through the notebooks and letters, my thoughts circled around and around. Sophie, Bert, Roger. Their faces appeared like a mental PowerPoint presentation, then disappeared. All of a sudden another face jumped out at me. That boy with the blond ponytail. It was true that Mom and I had never found him. But that didn't mean he couldn't have come back. And he certainly knew Bert, and probably Sophie, too. *He* could have rigged up everything.

As for the missing books and letters and albums, Sophie might have taken them back to Watoset with her. No, her doll-size suitcase was too small. Maybe Mom had taken them with her. After all, she had the blueprints in her bedroom closet. But I knew Mom would never do that without asking Great-Grandpa first. As a matter of fact, I could still be mistaken about the dates. It *was* possible there never had been anything in the panels after 1922. . . .

I shook my head in frustration and went back to sorting the letters. Who would want a lot of old letters anyway? Letters. I looked at the way each envelope had been ripped in half. It was funny how they were torn. . . .

YA-AAK! YA-AAK!

Jack Parrot! He sounded nearby, somewhere on the second floor. I quickly tiptoed up the stairs. There he was, perched on a hall light, his head cocked to one side as if he were waiting for me. He gave a shrill whistle. Jack was a tease all right. He was just leading me on. Well, he must be hungry and thirsty by now. I'd set food and water in a room. Then when he flew in for them, I'd shut the door and trap him. I tiptoed down the stairs again.

"What do parrots eat?" I called in to Great-Grandpa as I grabbed up my broom and crab net from the Bridge.

"Fruit," he grunted. "Seeds."

By the time I got everything together and had sneaked back up to the second floor, Jack Parrot was gone. I searched up and down the halls, but there was no sign of him. That parrot. He was smart, and no doubt about it. He had earned his breakfast. I set the bowl of water and a plate of grapes at the top of the stairs. Maybe it was just as well I hadn't found him. I had nothing to put him in.

I stuck my head in the Bridge door again. "I'm trying to catch Jack Parrot. Can you please help me find something to hold him?"

Great-Grandpa groaned. But he put down his paper and reached for his cane. "You're more trouble than you're worth. Months on end I don't go upstairs till bedtime, and here you've gotten me up there twice already this morning."

But as it turned out, he found me a birdcage in the attic and was as pleased about it as I was. The cage looked like the one in the pictures of Fanny Tillis. Looked like? It must be the very one.

I took it out to the kitchen and scrubbed and polished it. As I put the polish back under the sink, I noticed a can of yellow paint. I'd paint the cage and make it look really good. Halfway through the job, I realized I couldn't put a parrot in a freshly painted birdcage. How dumb could I be? Now I'd have to wait until it dried before catching Jack.

I finished the job, then joined Great-Grandpa on the Bridge. The minutes dragged the way they do in a boring class. Great-Grandpa read his newspaper all morning, every page, every line, every word. As far as I was concerned, it wasn't even much of a paper. It had all the wrong funnies. To pass the time, I started on Roger's mountain man book. But the storm distracted me. The rain hurled itself against the Bridge windows, retreated, then attacked again. I had heard the expression "howling wind" before but never knew that's just what it did. The seal rocks were gone from view. I took off my glasses and adjusted the telescope, but all I saw was gray rain hitting the gray water beneath a gray sky. Maybe the seals were around but there was no finding them.

Noonday dinner was Sophie's heated-up macaroni, vegetable salad, brown bread, and, for Great-Grandpa, baked beans. If I lived in Maine forever, I would never get used to baked beans. After dinner, Great-Grandpa took his afternoon nap in his chair on the Bridge. But not me. I read some more. I checked the birdcage (still wet). I had just started a handwritten letter to my friend Sarah when Dash set up a terrible barking outside the Bridge door. Great-Grandpa moaned in his sleep and flailed his arms around. I froze, pen in hand, my eyes glued to the opening door.

"Hello in there. Are you all right?" It was Doug Tate.

He stepped into the room, a big grin on his face.

"Oh, Mr. Tate, you came." I jumped up from my chair to greet him. Hooray! Roger had believed me after all.

"The Coombs boy insisted you needed help. I didn't have the nerve to ask Bert to bring me, so I used my Boston Whaler. It was some wild trip, let me tell you." Mr. Tate still had on his rain slicker, and the water streamed off him. Even his hair was damp, and I could see it spring back into curls the way mine does when it's wet. Only on a man it looks good.

"What are you talking about, Douglas?" Great-Grandpa was still struggling out of his nap.

"It was me, Great-Grandpa. I sent a message to Mr. Tate through Roger that we needed him."

"Nonsense, we're fine. And can manage for ourselves." Great-Grandpa was awake now. And mad.

"What do you mean, fine? I come out in this god-awful storm because I'm told you're in trouble. Now you say it's nonsense?" Mr. Tate sounded annoyed.

I tried to make peace. "But we do need you. I mean, we are in trouble. It's just that Great-Grandpa thinks if anyone hears what happened to us, they'll say he's crazy. But I was here and saw everything, too."

Mr. Tate took off his slicker and hung it over a chair where it dripped little puddles on the floor. "This isn't getting us anywhere. Tell me what's going on, and begin at the beginning, Kim."

So I did. Starting with the missing diaries and notebooks

and albums, through finding Jack Parrot, hearing the music, seeing the flashing lights, and ending up with the letters and mail and forgeries we found in Sophie's room.

Great-Grandpa didn't say a word. I could see he was getting crosser and crosser. But I didn't care. We *were* in trouble and needed help. Besides, Mr. Tate was almost like family. Hadn't his Uncle Alfred built The Anchorage in the first place?

Mr. Tate just sat and listened. Until I got to the part about Sophie. "You mean Sophie's selling things and forging Uncle Lester's name to the checks?" he interrupted, half standing up.

"It 'pears so, though I reckon the problem is betwixt Sophie and me." Great-Grandpa shot me a dark look.

Mr. Tate ran his fingers through his damp curly hair. "What is Sophie selling? How much money is she getting?"

Great-Grandpa's mouth was in a tight line. It was obvious he wasn't going to answer.

"We don't know what she's selling, but she's getting a lot of money for it. Fifteen hundred dollars," I said instead.

"Fifteen hundred dollars!" Mr. Tate pulled his chair closer to mine. His eyes behind his glasses were serious. "Did you find the missing blueprints and notebooks in Sophie's room?"

"No, Great-Grandpa was so upset we never finished looking."

Mr. Tate relaxed back in his chair and grinned. "I bet they're all right in Sophie's room. Why don't I take a look?

If I can find out what Sophie's selling, Uncle Lester, it would give you something definite to go on."

"I don't approve. Still, you got a point. And it does gnaw at me to know what Sophie's up to," Great-Grandpa agreed.

Mr. Tate stood up. "Who knows, other things might turn up besides the blueprints and diaries." He squeezed my shoulder as he headed for the door. "I'll be right back."

It wasn't until Mr. Tate left the Bridge that the word "blueprints" registered on me. Twice Mr. Tate had referred to the blueprints as missing. Who had said anything about missing blueprints? Not I. After all, I knew where they were. Right on Mom's closet shelf. Had Great-Grandpa mentioned the blueprints? I stared out the window trying to think. But so much had happened I just couldn't remember.

EIGHTEEN

A Broken Connection

Great-Grandpa had gone back to his newspaper and was really concentrating. His forehead frowned into furrows as his eyes moved from line to line. Should I say anything about Mr. Tate and the blueprints? I'd better not. Great-Grandpa was still mad at me for getting Mr. Tate out to Shag Island in the first place. For once I'd try to keep my mouth shut. I opened my Jim Bridger biography and began to read.

But Great-Grandpa's power of concentration was better than mine. I couldn't keep my mind on anything. I stood up and wandered over to the window. What a furious storm. Two terns flying into the wind were blown almost backwards. Mr. Tate must have had a terrible trip out. Mr. Tate. My thoughts kept backtracking to Doug Tate and why he was so interested in Sophie. Maybe pacing would help me think. I mentally marked off a section of the

Bridge floor and drew a line with the toe of my sneaker. One, two, three, go. Fifteen steps to the bookcase. Fifteen steps back. About face, and march to the bookcase again.

"For Christmas' sake, what are you doing?" Great-Grandpa demanded. It wasn't so much a question as an expletive. I know expletive means swearing, but I figured this was as close to swearing as Great-Grandpa usually got. At least in front of me.

I stopped in mid-step. "Pacing. I'm trying to think."

"Does it help?"

"No," I had to admit.

"Then set." Great-Grandpa snapped his newspaper for emphasis.

But I was too churned up to sit. I headed for the door.

Great-Grandpa peered over his paper. "Now where are you going?"

"To the bathroom."

"Good. Take your time."

As soon as I got upstairs, I went to the bathroom. Just so I wouldn't make myself out to be a liar. Then I headed for Sophie's room. I knocked on the closed door. "It's me, Kim. Can I come in?"

Before Mr. Tate could answer, I opened the door. The first thing I saw was Jack Parrot. He was perched on the footboard of Sophie's bed. When I came in, he fluttered his wings and danced a few steps. It was like a special greeting. The second thing I noticed was Mr. Tate bent over Sophie's bottom bureau drawer. Who had said anything about going through her bureau? The other drawers were open, too, and jumbo-sized blouses and sweaters lay every which way. And the desk was a mess. Papers were scattered all over.

Mr. Tate whirled around. His face was flushed under his tan, and he frowned. For just a second. Then he smiled his handsome smile. "I'm not having much luck," he said with a laugh. "Sophie's certainly up to something, but I can't figure out what it is. And I haven't been able to find the blueprints or any of the missing things."

I hadn't decided whether or not to tell Mr. Tate where the blueprints were. But his nervousness settled it. "That's the bird Great-Grandpa and I told you about," I said instead.

We both looked at Jack Parrot. It was as if he understood. He bent his head and scraped his beak against the footboard, just like an actor taking a bow. He was a charming showoff.

"He must have flown in a window somewhere." Mr. Tate shoved the drawer shut with his foot.

I tried not to show my surprise. From what I had seen, Maine birds were pretty much like New York birds except there were more gulls and fewer pigeons. But even to a non-bird-watcher like me, the idea of a big gray bird with a yellow face and long tail feathers flying in an Anchorage window seemed crazy.

"Yeah, you're probably right," I answered, congratulating myself on how I was learning to keep my mouth shut.

Mr. Tate wasn't listening anyway. He was rummaging in Sophie's closet, first through her top shelf, then through her rack of dresses. As he stepped out of the closet, he looked worried. But when he saw me still watching him, he quickly smiled and moved back to the desk. He sat down and started to go through everything again, paper by paper. After a while I felt funny just standing there.

YA-AAK! Jack Parrot wanted a little attention. He moved back and forth across the footboard, bobbing his head up and down. He seemed content to stay where he was. It might be a good time to capture him. And the cage must be drier by now.

"I'm going to try to catch the bird, Mr. Tate. Can you please keep the door shut while I get my net?"

I closed the door behind me and ran downstairs for my crab net and broom. But by the time I got them and returned to Sophie's room the door was open and both Mr. Tate and Jack were gone. Where were they? I hadn't passed them on the stairs. I ran out into the hall and looked both ways. No Jack Parrot. But I noticed the bathroom door was shut. And I had left it open. That must be where Mr. Tate was. I went back into Sophie's room.

It was a disaster. For the first time, I felt sorry for Sophie. I knew how mad I'd be if people snooped in my room and pawed through my clothes. I tidied up the closet shelf, then the drawers. As I headed for the desk, I almost stepped on a little pile of dry bird droppings. That was too much. I fished around in the wastebasket and came up with two envelopes to use as a scooper. One was from the *Reader's Digest.* The other was from Merritt, Rogers, Inc., Boston. Wasn't that the company that had sent Sophie the $1,500? I looked at the envelope. Under the company name in the top-left corner it read: "House of Philately and Numismatics."

I stood absolutely still. Waiting. For what I wasn't sure. Then it began to come to me, like a wave starting out at sea and rolling in. "Philately." I could see the word on my vocabulary list. It came right after "parasite" and right before "philosophy." And it meant . . . it meant . . . stamp collecting. Wow, that was it! Sophie was selling stamps. It explained why all the envelopes from Great-Great-Grandfather's letters had been torn down the right-hand side. Sophie must have ripped all the stamps off the letters Great-Great-Grandfather had mailed home from his trips.

Quickly I cleaned up the bird droppings. I could hardly wait to tell Great-Grandpa. I didn't know much about stamps, but I knew those had to be valuable. Dad had given me all his old boyhood stamps and shown me in a book what they were worth. And think of Great-Great-Grandfather's stamps. They were from all over the world, and some of them were more than a hundred years old. Maybe Sophie had gotten the $1,500 for just one stamp.

As soon as I finished straightening up the desk, I grabbed my net and broom and raced down the stairs. To my surprise, Great-Grandpa and Mr. Tate and Dash were in the front hall.

". . . that I can't be more help, but I don't want to delay getting back." Mr. Tate had on his rain gear and looked ready to go. "I'll try to come out first thing tomorrow."

"I 'preciate your interest, Douglas, but I told you Kimball and I can manage fine," Great-Grandpa said.

My news about Sophie and the stamps would have to wait until Mr. Tate left. It was funny. I had been so glad to see him come. Now I was glad to see him go. I followed him to the front door.

"You know I'd stay if I could, Kim." Mr. Tate turned his charm on me.

"That's all right," I said fast. I didn't want him to change his mind. I even opened the door for him. A sweep of damp wind blew into the house, and I shivered. Water streamed from the downspouts on either side of the porch.

Bang-bang-bang. There was that racket again. The shutter Roger fixed must have come loose. Mr. Tate didn't seem to notice. He pulled on his hood and hunched up his shoulders. I followed him out to the front porch. He ran across the yard and down the cliff steps, his yellow rain slicker bobbing out of sight. Gone. Great-Grandpa and I were alone again. Somehow I didn't mind as much as I had before.

Bang-bang-bang. The shutter was slapping hard against the house. I stuck my head around the edge of the porch. By the time I saw where the shutter hook was hanging off, my hair was soaked. But it looked easy enough to fix.

"That dining-room shutter is loose again," I explained to Great-Grandpa as I pulled an old slicker out of the hall closet and slipped it on. It was stiff and smelled rubbery.

I took off my sneakers and ran outside barefoot. The wind tugged at me, and the rain pelted down hard as hail. Windshield wipers on my glasses would have come in handy.

First of all, I wanted to make sure Mr. Tate had got off okay. I ran to the top of the cliff stairs. Yes, there he was starting up his Boston Whaler with a burst of exhaust fumes. What a storm. It would be a bad trip. I watched the little boat slap its way toward the mainland. When it was finally swallowed up by the curtain of rain, I ran back to the dining-room window.

Standing on tiptoe, I grabbed the shutter. Just as I reached up to fix the hook, my attention was drawn to the shingles behind the shutter. Riveted, is more like it. The wire that ran up the side of the house had been cut. Not only cut, but a five- or six-inch section of wire had been taken right out. I fixed the shutter automatically, then backed away from the house and followed the line from the dining-room window all the way up to the roof. It led right to the radio antenna. The shock I felt was the same as when I was six and stuck a lamp plug and my finger into a socket at the same time. That is, stunned. If the line led from the dining-room window to the antenna, it had to mean the cut wire was connected to Great-Grandpa's radio.

NINETEEN

The Room with a Closet

I stood gaping at the wire until I realized the rain was running down my neck into my slicker. I raced back into the house. Great-Grandpa was sitting on the bottom step of the stairs, trying to get a tick off Dash.

"The radio wire by the dining-room window has been cut," I blurted out. I slipped out of my wet slicker and shook my head. The water sprayed off my hair like a dog's. That's one advantage to short hair. It dries fast.

Great-Grandpa's thick eyebrows arched up. "Are you certain? If that's so, I'd better take a look. I may have to splice it. Lemme have your foul-weather gear." He chucked Dash under the chin and then, leaning on his cane, heaved himself to his feet. He took a step forward, teetered, and almost fell. Before I could reach him, he steadied himself with his cane. He looked as bent as the gnarled apple tree by the back door. Probably the bad weather made his bones stiffen right up. And ache. But he never complained.

I helped him on with the slicker and even found an old hat to go with it. I opened the front door and waited on the porch while he slowly made his way to the dining-room window. He was frail enough for the wind to pick up and blow away. But he made it. After he looked everything over, he headed back to the house. But he didn't say a word until we were both inside and I had hung up his slicker and hat.

"Foolishness! Foolishness! With that wire cut, the radio will never work. And it can't be spliced. Now Charlie Wells will have to come all the way out to repair it."

Didn't Great-Grandpa understand? Someone had deliberately cut the wire. And the radio was our only link with the mainland. That and the leaky little rowboat on the back cove beach. When I was younger, I used to get claustrophobia in elevators. It's an awful feeling when the doors close. The walls seem to press in, and you're sure you'll never get out. All of a sudden I tightened up with that same feeling of being trapped. Only trapped on an island, not in an elevator.

"I s'pose you'd say Sophie cut out that section of wire," Great-Grandpa commented.

So he hadn't missed the point. But for once, I wasn't thinking of Sophie. Roger had fixed that shutter. Roger must have cut the wire. No, that was ridiculous. Of course Roger hadn't done it. But who had? The radio hadn't been used since Harvey called Mom. Sophie, Bert, Roger, Mr. Tate, Mr. Tate's clients, that blond boy, Great-Grandpa.

Everyone was a possibility. I tried to fight down my rising panic. Mom always told me to think of something else when I got in an elevator. But it was hard to do then, and it was hard to do now.

Sophie and the stamps. That's what I had been so excited about just a few minutes ago. I tried to work up the same excitement. "Sophie has been taking all the stamps off your father's old letters and selling them to that place in Boston, and that's what she's getting money for." I rattled on as if each word were hyphenated to the next.

"Huh?" Great-Grandpa cupped his ear as if he hadn't heard right.

I didn't blame him. I repeated myself. Slower.

This time I got a reaction. "Stamps. Father's stamps." Great-Grandpa spluttered. "Those envelopes were all ripped. Of course you're right. But for Sophie to steal them. If she had wanted them, I would have given them to her." Great-Grandpa was beginning to work himself into a rage. His face turned red. Even his long ears looked flushed. "On top of cashing my checks . . . forging my name . . . how could Sophie have been so deceitful? It's too much. . . ." He stopped, gasping for breath.

Good night, he looked like he was going to faint or have a heart attack or something. Just then the hall clock gonged once. Five thirty. "Supper," I said fast. "We ought to be cooking supper. Aren't you hungry? I'm starved." I was about as hungry as I am after a Thanksgiving turkey. But Great-Grandpa looked so terrible I'd have eaten Dash's dog food to distract him.

"Supper," he repeated. He pulled out his pocket watch. "You're right. It's past suppertime. We got to get at it." Whew, my diversionary tactics had worked.

The big kitchen was absolutely freezing. No wonder. The back door was wide open. The wind must have done it. I wouldn't let myself consider anything else. In New York I was used to deadbolt locks with chains and peepholes. Doors in The Anchorage didn't have any locks at all.

"I got a chill right through from going outside," Great-Grandpa said after I'd closed the back door. "I'd like my wool shawl that Sophie . . . *humph*, that Sophie . . . made for me. It's in my top dresser drawer. Go fetch it, will you please, whilst I start up the fire?"

Oh, brother, me go upstairs alone? Did I have to? If I didn't want Great-Grandpa to get pneumonia, I did. Besides, I was a big New York City girl, wasn't I, used to staying by myself at night, riding subways and bicycling in Central Park?

"Don't think, just keep going," I told myself as I marched upstairs. The slap of rain against the landing windows sounded like a hundred little drumbeats. I didn't look to the right or left. I just put one foot in front of the other all the way to Great-Grandpa's room.

I had already found the shawl and was just coming out of my room with a sweater for myself when I heard Jack Parrot shriek. Hard as it is to believe, I had forgotten all about him. He sounded nearby, but the cry was muffled, as if he were in a closet or behind a closed door. I quick pulled on my sweater and started up the hall.

YA-AAK. It was like a game of Hot and Cold. He sounded closer, almost as if he were in one of the other two rooms in our wing. But those two doors were shut and always had been.

YA-AAK. Jack *was* behind one of those closed doors. I opened the door of the room next to Great-Grandpa's. Cautiously. It was small without any windows, more like a cell than a room. Piles of furniture were stacked along one wall. I made my way to what looked like a standing lamp by the door and fumbled for the switch. A weak yellow light blinked on. Immediately, there was a banging crash from the far corner of the room, and Jack Parrot took off with a flapping of his strong wings. He flew past my head and out the open door. I would have screamed, but my throat locked tight. Even though I had expected to find Jack, the sudden way he bombed past me caved my knees in.

How in the world had Jack got shut in here? Last time I had seen Jack, he had been with Mr. Tate in Sophie's room. The only explanation I could think of was that Jack had followed Mr. Tate in here, and Mr. Tate had closed the door on him. Maybe there was something in the room that Mr. Tate was looking for. The idea interested me enough so that I stopped shaking and started poking around. The room was full of old baby furniture and broken wicker chairs and tables. I moved the standing lamp as far into the room as the wire would stretch and tipped the lampshade so I could see better. A three-legged chair lay on the floor. That must have been the crash I heard. Jack had probably knocked it over when he took off.

A closet door was open, but the closet was empty. There wasn't even a pole to hang clothes on. For such a small room, the closet was awfully big. It ran the whole width of one wall and was all paneled in some kind of dark wood. And it had a funny rolltop door, like a garage door that pulls down from overhead. I stood in front of the closet, grabbed the handle, and rolled the door down. The loud rattling sound of it startled me.

I had to be out of my mind. What was I doing, snooping around in this weird little room? I backed away from the closet. If only Jack hadn't flown out. He was almost human, and right now I wanted human company very badly. What a strange house, full of strange goings-on. I turned off the lamp and ran from the room, yanking the door shut behind me. I rushed down the stairs and out to the kitchen and the safety of Great-Grandpa, Dash, and a warm wood fire.

TWENTY

Blueprint to Danger

Almost as soon as we finished supper, Great-Grandpa and I went upstairs. Great-Grandpa was still upset about Sophie, and I could see he was tired and ready for bed. And I had an idea in the back of my mind.

"Mom was studying The Anchorage blueprints in her room. I'd like to take a look at them, too. I still get lost in this place." I laughed as if it were a big joke. It was a pretty feeble laugh, but Great-Grandpa didn't seem to notice.

"Wasn't Douglas concerned about some blueprints?" Great-Grandpa asked without much interest.

"Oh . . . I don't know . . . I guess so," I hedged. Mr. Tate had been concerned all right. Too concerned. I wanted to check them over myself before I said anything to Great-Grandpa about finding Jack Parrot in that dark little room. If I put my mind to it, maybe I could figure this out on my own, the way I had with Sophie and the stamps.

After I picked up the blueprints from Mom's room, Great-Grandpa and I made careful arrangements for the night. We made sure Dash lay down between our two bedrooms. We turned on the hall light and left our doors open. It was my idea to set up a signal system. We each had a bell by our beds to ring if we needed anything. Great-Grandpa said it was silly, but I wasn't going to take any chances. I decided not to undress. No Chinese music and flashing lights were going to catch me unprepared this time.

From across the hall I heard Great-Grandpa get ready for bed, talking to himself the whole time. Probably about Sophie. He opened and slammed drawers, then his closet door. After he finished in the bathroom, I heard his bed creak as he climbed on it. A few minutes later it creaked again as he climbed off it. He was restless, too.

The storm blew on. The wind had begun to die down, but it still whined and whistled as if crying to get in the house. I tried to ignore it as I spread out the blueprints on my bed and knelt on the floor to study them. They weren't all that easy to figure out. First I had to find the second-floor plans. Which looked exactly like the third-floor plans. Then I had to locate the main staircase. From there I worked up one hall and down another. It was like a maze, only inside out. After a few wrong turns, I found Great-Grandpa's room and mine right across from it, as well as the other two rooms that made up our wing. The room next to my bedroom was big, about the same size as mine. But the room next to Great-Grandpa's bedroom, the room where I had found Jack Parrot, was really tiny.

There was something else weird. The blueprints showed a fifth room. It was between the tiny room and Great-Grandpa's room. But where was the door to it? There were only four doors in the hallway. As I studied the floor plan, I had the same feeling I get when I suddenly see the solution to a complicated math problem. Step one leads to step two leads to step three. Therefore: conclusion. I breathed on my glasses and cleaned them with my shirttail. I just knew I was close to some kind of conclusion.

I walked my fingers on the blueprint from my bedroom, up the hall, and to the door of the room where I had found Jack Parrot. I marched them through the door and over to the big closet. And I found what I was looking for. On the plans a door led from the closet into the fifth room. I hadn't noticed a door in the empty closet. But the back wall had been paneled in dark wood. I bet one of those panels swung in, just like the secret panels on the staircase landing. *Yes!* I grabbed my pillow and threw it into the air. That fifth room just had to be the answer. Maybe Great-Grandpa knew all about it.

I ran out into the hall, leaped over a sleeping Dash, and raced into Great-Grandpa's room with the blueprint. He was seated in a chair dressed in pajamas with his false teeth out. He wasn't reading or napping or doing anything. He was just staring at the floor.

"Look what I found. A secret room right here in our

wing." I pointed to the blueprint. "See, behind this closet. Do you know what's in it?"

Great-Grandpa studied the blueprint I held out to him. Then he looked up at me. Sheepishly. "I guess I need my glasses," he said as if he were ashamed to admit it. At ninety-three.

"That room *is* queer. I don't know anything about it," he said after I'd gotten his glasses. "It may be a mistake in the plans. Still, we'd better take a look for ourselves. Wait outside for a minute."

Out in the hall I danced up and down with impatience. My excitement was contagious. Dash didn't get up, but he thumped his long tail on the floor. Then Great-Grandpa came out, wearing his bathrobe and slippers and carrying a flashlight. His teeth were back in. Dignity, that's what Great-Grandpa had, teeth or no teeth.

Poor Dash. He had counted on being settled for the night. Now here was Great-Grandpa up and walking around. Dash struggled to his feet. Where Great-Grandpa went, Dash went.

The standing lamp was right where I had left it, in the middle of the room. I turned it on. Its lampshade was still tilted toward the empty closet.

"I figure one of those back panels in the closet opens into the secret room," I said.

Great-Grandpa nodded. He turned on his flashlight, and led the way into the closet. We were Lewis and Clark sighting the Pacific. This was it. Together we pressed and prodded the panels. The next to last one on the right was the magic number. It swung in easily. The opening was high enough to pass through upright. We stepped into a good-sized room, just as the blueprints promised.

"Flash your light around," I said. I don't know what I expected, but it had to be something fantastic. Great-Grandpa was excited, too. His hand shook as he shone the light from one end of the room to the other. I couldn't believe it. It was just a storeroom, full of stuff like the rest of The Anchorage. Crates and barrels, statues, china bowls and vases, rolled-up rugs, trunks, a pile of old swords and canes, and dusty furniture were piled every which way. What a letdown!

But Great-Grandpa had gone into some kind of shock. He started to breathe so hard I could hear his chest wheeze. "Father's curios . . . the whole room . . . all these years . . ."

"What do you mean?" I asked.

But he didn't answer. He walked across the room toward a big barrel with "1923" stenciled on the side. The top had been pried open. Bits of packing straw and a few pieces of china lay uncovered. Great-Grandpa pulled out a tall, long-necked pitcher. "Father's curios. I can't believe it. . . ."

"What do you mean, curios?" I demanded.

"Every Maine shipmaster's home had a curiosity room, full of curios and treasures brought back from abroad," Great-Grandpa said in a funny, strained voice. "The china dishes in the kitchen are all that Father ever left. I always wondered why there wasn't more. But here everything is, hidden away. I don't understand."

He swung his flashlight the length of the room again. I noticed a statue of a horse on a long table. It looked like one I had seen at the Metropolitan Museum of Art in New York. And there was a strange-looking suit of armor. And a big seated Buddha. Maybe this stuff was more than just junk. Then I saw something next to the horse that really jolted me. A laptop with speakers!

"Let me have your flashlight," I said to Great-Grandpa. Shining the light on the table, I inspected the laptop. I turned it on.

The sound of the light tinkling chimes shouldn't have been a shock, but it was. Shock enough to start my heart to thumping in my chest. Shock enough for Great-Grandpa to gasp out loud. We looked at each other without saying a word. We didn't need to. I clicked the music off. The silence was so sudden, we could hear the sounds of the storm even in the windowless room. It seemed to wail through the attic above us.

So this room *did* have some answers after all. I put the flashlight on the table and began to poke around. Great-Grandpa did, too. But I was interested in more than his father's curios.

"Look at this," I cried out. Stacked on top of a crate were the missing letters and notebooks and albums: 1923, 1924, 1925. All of them. So I had been right. Someone had taken them. And hidden them here. There was even a set of Anchorage blueprints. Mine was still back in Great-Grandpa's room, I knew. This must be a second set. Where had it come from? The solution to my math problem was as skittery as a crab in a tidepool. First it was right in my grasp; then it scooted away.

I opened the first notebook. March 1923. "Does the year 1923 mean anything to you, Great-Grandpa?" I asked.

He frowned. "The year 1923? Well, let's see . . . 1923 . . . that was the year Father and his crew were captured by pirates off the coast of Hainan, China. Father escaped, but when he returned, he started to talk of retirement. It must have been a terrible experience. He would never discuss it."

"You'll find the whole story right in that diary," said a quiet voice. It came from behind us. Someone was standing in the doorway of the closet.

I spun around. But all I could see was the sun-bright glare of a flashlight aimed right in my eyes. There was no way to make out who was behind it. But whoever it was could see us, for sure.

TWENTY-ONE

The Captain's Secret

It was as if my body had turned to Jell-O and my brains to the whipped cream on top. I stared into the light without a thought in my head.

But Great-Grandpa was fantastic. "Well, who's there?" he barked, just as if he were on top of the situation.

There was a long silence. Then the light moved toward us until it was so blinding, I had to shade my eyes. "It's me," came the reply. "Douglas Tate."

But Douglas Tate was gone. I had seen his boat leave.

Mr. Tate held the flashlight under his chin. He was smiling, but the effect was really weird. His head looked disconnected from his body, like a grinning Halloween mask, and the light reflected off his glasses so I couldn't see his eyes. The hairs on the back of my neck prickled. Stood on end, was more like it.

"What are you doing here?" Great-Grandpa demanded.

"I was worried about you two and thought I'd better

come back after all," Mr. Tate answered almost too easily.

I was tongue-tied. I couldn't have said anything if I wanted to. But at least my adrenaline had started pumping. I could feel it clear the whipped cream from my head. How had Mr. Tate found us? There was no way he had come back to help us, and just happened to find us here.

Great-Grandpa didn't swallow his story either. "This room, full of Father's curios, how does it concern you, Douglas?"

"Why, I'm the one who discovered it, Uncle Lester. I'd say that's reason enough for concern."

If Mr. Tate had discovered it, then *he* had set up that Chinese music.

Great-Grandpa was as stunned by his answer as I was. "You found these things in *my* house? What are you talking about, Douglas?"

Mr. Tate stepped farther into the room. "Let's just say it was happenstance."

"If you know so much about my house, then tell me how Father's curios got to be put away in here." Great-Grandpa's jaw was set in a stubborn line.

"I can tell you all right, Uncle Lester. But you may not want to hear it. Your father didn't buy these treasures abroad, he stole them. That's why he had Uncle Alfred design this special room in The Anchorage right behind his bedroom. It was a good place to store everything in secret." Mr. Tate's voice was pleasant.

But not Great-Grandpa's. He thumped his cane on the floor. "Father would never do such a thing."

Great-Grandpa's thoughts went one way. Mine went another. Mr. Tate must have taken the diaries and albums and letters and hidden them here. But how had he found this room in the first place?

The sound of my own voice startled me. I hadn't realized I had asked the question aloud until I heard it.

"Uncle Alfred had a set of Anchorage blueprints that I found last winter when I cleaned out his old files," Mr. Tate answered, still pleasant. "I gave the plans a quick once-over and noticed this big room with no outside door. It seemed odd. So when Uncle Lester was in the hospital last March, I took the opportunity to come over and check it out. And this is what I found." He swung his flashlight the length of the room, lingering on one dusty treasure after another.

I didn't bother to look. The puzzle was beginning to fall into place. Mr. Tate had wanted our set of blueprints because he was afraid we would find this room, too. Which we had.

"You can imagine the scare I had when you found all those books and letters and blueprints in those staircase shelves, Kim," Mr. Tate continued. "I didn't even know they existed. But I was certain they would give away the secret of this room. Since 1923 was stamped on some of these crates, I figured that was the year the captain had . . . ah . . . acquired his curios. I simply removed everything from the staircase shelves after 1922 to make sure no one would read them and trace down this room too. The only loose end is that second set of blueprints I haven't been able to find. It's not hard to guess that you two have it."

I didn't say a word. And hoped Great-Grandpa wouldn't either. I needn't have worried. Great-Grandpa had something else on his mind. "It was when I got back from the hospital that the Chinese music started. And the flashing lights at night," he said. He rubbed his mustache the way he does when he's thinking.

Like everyone else, Mr. Tate must have known how Great-Great-Grandfather was haunted by Chinese ghosts. So he had tried to drive Great-Grandpa crazy the same way. Talk about a sleaze.

But Mr. Tate seemed pleased with himself. "The lights and music and bird were quite ingenious, don't you think? Only one thing didn't work out just right. Bert happened to mention to me that Kim was going back to New York with her mother. So I set up the music and the lights and released the bird in your bedroom, Lester. By the time I found out Kim wasn't going after all, it was too late to change my plans. Still, it was all pretty effective. A little more pressure, and you'd have been safely committed. Then, with The Anchorage sold, I would have moved all these things out with the rest of your furniture."

The bird. Of course. Mr. Tate had brought out the big camera case yesterday. Jack Parrot must have been inside. All of a sudden I was boiling mad. And if I was mad, think how Great-Grandpa must feel. He was sure to blow his stack.

But he surprised me. He didn't say anything, He just walked over to a wooden screen propped against the wall.

Absentmindedly, he traced around its carved design. "You had it planned out real careful, Douglas. Even down to cutting out that section of wire. I can believe all of it. All except that Father stole these things," he said.

"But it's true." Mr. Tate smiled. "You know when the Chinese pirates lured your father's ship onto the rocks? The story has an ending you never heard. It's all in that diary Kim is holding. Your father and his crew escaped, all right, but they took everything with them they could, all the loot the pirates had stolen over the years. And here it is."

"But Father never said—"

"Of course he didn't. And being a basically moral man, he never enjoyed it either, I'm sure. Why, his conscience bothered him right to the end. But you know all about his Chinese ghosts." Mr. Tate's laugh was almost a sneer. "Now a guilty conscience will never bother me. I'll just sell it all, sit back, and enjoy the money."

The word "sell" nudged a memory. Mr. Tate had been so uptight about what Sophie was selling. Now I could see why.

"You didn't come back to help us at all. You were afraid Sophie had gotten hold of the blueprints and found this room. You just wanted to make sure Sophie wasn't selling all this stuff." The words popped out before I remembered I was going to keep my mouth shut.

"Sophie is a foolish old woman," Mr. Tate declared. "I *was* worried she had found this room. But I didn't have enough time to check earlier, so I circled back. But I can see nothing's missing. I know every piece, and it's all here.

Sophie must be selling your fine collection of antlers, Uncle Lester." Mr. Tate laughed.

"She's selling Father's stamps," Great-Grandpa said.

"Stamps? Why, for Sophie, that's pretty imaginative." Mr. Tate laughed again.

It was the laugh that finished me. Everyone was robbing Great-Grandpa blind and treating it as a big joke.

"You're terrible. How could you do this to Great-Grandpa?" I rushed at Mr. Tate and gave him a hard push. I took him by surprise. He dropped his flashlight and fell back against a stack of crates.

"Run!" I screamed at Great-Grandpa.

But before I even made it to the door, Mr. Tate overtook me. He grabbed me by the waist of my jeans and pulled me right off my feet.

"Help!"

I kicked out with all my might and swung my fists as hard as I could. But Mr. Tate dangled me at harmless arm's length.

"That settles it." Mr. Tate wasn't laughing now. Still holding on to me, he reached Great-Grandpa in a couple of long strides and seized his arm. He shoved the two of us up against the wall. The flashlight lay on the floor where it had fallen, beaming across the room. In its uneven light, Mr. Tate towered above us. His height made Great-Grandpa look smaller than ever. And shaken. I was shaken, too. We were backed up against the wall like a couple of mice cornered by a cat. And the cat loomed between us and the door.

TWENTY-TWO

Night of Terror

I had to face it. There was no way Great-Grandpa and I could overpower a six-foot-two man who was really uptight. Mr. Tate was breathing hard and looked worried. That was bad. I knew he was worried about what to do with Great-Grandpa and me.

"Okay." He sounded as if he had made a decision. He reached down and picked up something from the floor. He held it in the beam of the flashlight so we could see it. A sword. The handle was gold and had bright stones in it, as if it was for decoration. But it also had a long curving blade, as if it meant business.

"The sword is a little melodramatic, I admit, but I'll use it if I have to," Mr. Tate said. "I'm not going to be crossed up now by an old man and a ten-year-old child."

"Twelve," I corrected him. As if it mattered.

Great-Grandpa shook his head. "You're wicked, Douglas. Wicked."

Mr. Tate ignored both of us. "All right, we're going downstairs. You first, Lester, through the door. C'mon, get going."

He bent down and retrieved his flashlight as we headed for the door. When we came out through the closet, Dash was waiting for us curled up on an old crib mattress. He sat up when he saw us and began to scratch his ear furiously. Some watchdog.

We started down the hall. Great-Grandpa went first, with Dash beside him, then me, followed by Mr. Tate with his sword. I was sure he would never use it, but I wasn't about to put my theory to the test.

As we came down the stairs, I saw Jack Parrot. He was asleep on the newel post. When he heard us, he fluttered off his perch. Then he settled back down again, tucking his head under his wing. He wasn't any better than Dash. Weren't parrots supposed to talk? He might have at least squawked a warning.

"Go through the kitchen and hurry up," Mr. Tate called out impatiently.

"It's the best I can do," Great-Grandpa snapped. What guts. No one was going to push *him* around.

"Now out the back door."

Outside in this storm? It would be too much for Great-Grandpa. He had only his bathrobe and slippers on. We huddled in the doorway, looking out at the wild night. The wind had let up some, but the rain was coming down as hard as ever.

"Hold this searchlight at Lester's feet so he can see." Mr. Tate stuck the big flashlight in my hand. "We're going down to the back cove, Lester. Get started." Mr. Tate was beginning to sound edgy. I didn't like it. The more nervous he was, the worse it promised to be for Great Grandpa and me. The palms of my hands turned so cold and sweaty I could hardly hold the flashlight.

As soon as we stepped outside, the force of the wind stopped Great-Grandpa in his tracks. I bumped into him. Mr. Tate in turn bumped into me. With a curse. I took Great-Grandpa's arm to help him. His whole body was trembling. Or maybe it was me who was trembling. It didn't matter. We were a shaky pair as we started across the backyard. Dash whimpered in the doorway behind us. He was afraid to leave the house but, at the same time, afraid to let Great-Grandpa out of his sight.

Our progress was slow. Dash made up his mind to join us but stuck so close to Great-Grandpa he was a real hazard underfoot. I held the flashlight. Mr. Tate held the sword. There had to be some way one would offset the other. But Mr. Tate had only himself to think about. And I had Great-Grandpa. He had trouble just maneuvering the path, let alone trying to run, hide, jump Mr. Tate, make it back to the house, or do any of the other things that might get us out of this.

Mr. Tate tapped me on the shoulder. "Shine your light into that tree." He wanted us to climb a tree? No, he pointed out a strobe light rigged up to a branch. It was directed right into what had to be Great-Grandpa's window.

"I was dumb enough to think the flashing lights were from Bert Smith's boat," I said.

"Bert Smith doesn't have the sense to come in out of the rain." Mr. Tate gave his short bark of a laugh. "Neither do we, so it seems. Move faster. I'm getting soaked."

We all were. My hair was plastered to my face, and the driving rain blurred my glasses. I was wet through, and then some. Where the flashlight shone on Great-Grandpa's feet, I saw his slippers were globs of mud and the water poured off the hem of his bathrobe. Dash's long tail curved down instead of up as he limped along. The whole scene was out of a nightmare. It wasn't really happening. The sun would shine through my window and wake me up. After breakfast Mom and I would walk along the water's edge, looking for shells and sea glass.

But it *was* happening, and it was a long, painful trek down to the cove beach. Great-Grandpa slipped on the first step and would have fallen if I hadn't grabbed him. Mr. Tate finally ended up nudging him down from step to step. Great-Grandpa protested at every bump. Me, too. If empathy means feeling for someone else, empathy for Great-Grandpa was what I had.

Then we were at the bottom, on the little cove beach. The wind whined through the trees and boiled up the black bay into white-topped curls. Dash circled around us whimpering, his head bowed against the storm. Great-Grandpa's head was bowed, too, and he seemed dazed. I

felt dazed myself. It was as if the rain had soaked every logical thought through my head like it was a strainer. I realized we were in bad shape, Great-Grandpa and me. But
beyond that, I only knew I was drenched and freezing.

"Give me the flashlight." Mr. Tate's voice was gentle.

Encouraged, I handed it to him. He turned its light
toward the water. The bay was in a fury. Angry waves
slapped on the pebbly beach, then retreated with a suck-
ing hiss. I saw the old rowboat pulled up just beyond the
waterline, with Mr. Tate's Boston Whaler next to it. Dash
followed the beam of light, too. He walked over to the
Whaler, lifted his leg, and wet on it.

"That damned dog!" Mr. Tate aimed a kick at Dash.
"He can go, too."

Go where? Out in the Whaler? But it was too stormy.
And dark.

"Now both of you get in the rowboat," Mr. Tate directed.

He had to be crazy. The rowboat was a sieve. Great-
Grandpa couldn't swim, and I could barely stay afloat. I
stared at Mr. Tate with my mouth hanging open.

"Hurry up. Get in the boat." He slashed his sword
through the air. A pulse pounded in my throat. There was
no counting on Mr. Tate not to use the sword now. It was
like walking in on a burglar. A trapped burglar is unpre-
dictable. And dangerous. And Mr. Tate was so tense the
top of his head was ready to blow off.

I approached the rowboat. But I couldn't get in. I just
looked at it. That wasn't good enough for Mr. Tate. He

gave me a shove from behind that sent me sprawling into the boat. I scraped my hands and knees as I hit the splintery bottom. I quick grabbed the gunwales to regain my balance. But before I could get off my knees, Mr. Tate lifted Great-Grandpa into the other end of the boat. He landed with a groan.

"Great-Grandpa." I crawled toward him. But before I could reach him, a heavy body hit me square on, knocking the breath right out of me. I fell on my side as sharp nails dug into me. It was Dash.

"Help!" I screamed. "Help!"

There was the sudden motion of the boat sliding toward the water. I struggled to get Dash off me.

"Stop! Help!" I cried. My face was salty wet. Whether it was rain or tears or salt water I didn't know. I lay where I had fallen, the full weight of Dash on top of me, clawing and scratching to get out. Great-Grandpa was slumped in the stern as the boat hit the water. The night was a black curtain of rain and wind drawn around us. "Help!" I screamed again. "Help!"

Mr. Tate was still behind us, pushing us farther out. He was knee-deep, then waist-deep. Mom had said the shoreline dropped off sharply. Mr. Tate must have known that. With a final shove he let go of the boat, and we bobbed free as a cork.

Oars. There were oars somewhere in the boat. I remembered them. With both hands and all my strength, I pushed Dash off me and frantically scrambled around the boat. But there were no oars. All I felt was the gush of water pumping into the leaky bottom.

"We got to do something. We'll sink," Great-Grandpa called.

We lurched and tossed on the waves. The wind had swung us around so that I wasn't sure which direction was land and which was out to sea.

"Help!" I shrieked.

Aaarrrooo! Aaarrrooo! Aaarrrooo! Dash had climbed up on the seat and was howling into the night.

The level of the water was rising in the boat so that it lapped around the seat of my pants. It was cold and wet enough to shock me into action. I jumped up on the seat beside Dash and began to scoop out the water with my cupped hands. Over and over until my aching arms felt disconnected from my body. But the boat was filling faster than I could ever bail. We were listing. It was hopeless. I made my way toward the stern. When I reached Great-Grandpa, I threw my arms around him and buried my head in his shoulder. He hugged me tight as I squeezed my eyes shut. I heard Dash barking as if from a great distance. I was beyond crying. Almost beyond caring.

TWENTY-THREE

Dash the Hero

"A light."

Had I heard Great-Grandpa right? With Dash barking and the wind and rain beating at us, it was hard to hear anything at all. I raised my head from Great-Grandpa's shoulder. The rain blurred my glasses, but I could see a round yellow glow. There *was* a light. And it was coming closer.

"Help!" I screamed. "Help!"

Now I could hear the putt-putt of a motorboat. Then the light was right on top of us, circling around.

"A rope! A towrope!" a man's voice shouted. Right away I knew it wasn't Mr. Tate. Beyond that, I didn't care if it was Jack the Ripper.

A rope came whipping through the air and splashed in the bottom of our boat. Great-Grandpa couldn't handle the situation. It was up to me. I reached for the rope.

Should I hold it? No, I'd better tie it. Awkwardly I made my way to the bow. Past Dash. Over the seat. Careful as I was, water poured over the side. Easy, or the boat will swamp. Tie the rope. Quick! But it was wet and hard to knot. There. I tried to inch my way back to the middle of the boat, but more water splashed in.

"We're sinking!" I shrieked.

The man yelled back, but I couldn't hear him. Then there was a thud as something landed in our boat. I grabbed it and held it up to the beam of his searchlight. It looked like a bicycle pump. That's what it was. A pump! It shouldn't be hard to work.

It wasn't. I began to pump. And pump some more. I pumped all the way in to shore. I didn't think about anything, couldn't think about anything, but pumping. Not who was towing us in. Or where he had come from. Just up and down, up and down. The swish of water squirting over the side of the boat was about the greatest sound I ever heard.

Then I felt the nudge of our bow against the stern of the towboat. A man jumped into the water beside us and pulled us the last few feet to shore. Then we were scraping across the rocky beach. Still I pumped. I just had to bail out every drop of water.

"You can stop now." The man stood right next to me, shining his flashlight into our boat. But I could still see a couple of inches of water left. I couldn't stop.

The man turned his light on Great-Grandpa. Great-

Grandpa's eyes were open, but the pale look of him brought me up short. I dropped the pump and rushed to his side.

"Great-Grandpa, are you all right?"

He turned his head and looked at me. He must have seen how worried I was. He didn't say anything, but he gave me that quick wink of his and tried to smile. What a relief. But it was still raining, and the wind was like Mr. Tate's sword cutting through us. We had to get out of here. What if Mr. Tate knew we were safe?

But when I climbed out of the boat, I was so stiff I could hardly move. Was there such a thing as lockjaw of the bones? If there was, I had it. Dash stood on the seat whining. His eyes begged me to help him. I reached over and lifted him to the ground.

Then I turned back to Great-Grandpa. But our rescuer had already put his flashlight down and was giving Great-Grandpa a hand out of the boat. The man wore a poncho. His feet were bare. And when he leaned over, I saw a straggly, wet ponytail in the beam of his flashlight. It was the boy from the lobster shed I had met on my first day in Maine, the same boy I had seen twice already on the island. Somehow it didn't surprise me. Maybe I was beyond surprise.

"Now listen to me." The boy talked loud and slow as if we were both deaf. Or idiots. "I'm gonna get you to a dry place as fast as I can. I don't want that crazy up there to see us. Do you understand?"

I nodded. I understood enough to know I didn't want that crazy up there to see us either. And "dry" sounded fantastic.

I did just what he told me. Between us, we supported Great-Grandpa and made our way down the beach in the opposite direction from The Anchorage. Then we turned toward the woods and started climbing. Dash, too. I could hear him wheezing along behind us.

The pine trees grew thicker. Though they acted as giant umbrellas against the rain, their sharp needles scratched and snapped in our faces. Gnarled roots and mossy rocks made the going slippery. We twisted and turned our slow way through the woods. Then we stopped.

"Here we are," the boy said.

Where? There wasn't even a clearing. Then in the beam of the flashlight, I saw it. Some sort of shed, its roof covered with pine boughs. We bent down and entered a tiny little house with tiny little furniture. It was weird, like something out of Snow White and the Seven Dwarfs. But it was warm. And dry. The boy and I eased Great-Grandpa into a low chair. Then the boy lit a kerosene lamp.

"I'll heat up some coffee and get the old man in dry clothes." The boy still spoke slowly, the way I do when someone doesn't understand English. It was just as well. My mind was working about half a sentence behind what he was saying.

First he lit a Sterno can and put a coffee pot on it. Then he got Great-Grandpa out of his clothes and into a sweater and a pair of much-too-big jeans. I wanted to help, but I was shaking all over, and my own clothes had congealed on me like wet plastic. I must have looked as miserable as I felt.

"Here, put these on." The boy unzipped his duffel bag. It was the same duffel bag I had seen Bert hand him on the dock. The boy tossed a pair of jeans and a sweatshirt at me. Then he turned his back so I could change. Not that seeing me was such a thrill, but I was grateful. The water dripped off my hair and down my back as I dropped my soggy clothes on the floor. I rubbed myself with the sweatshirt. Then I pulled on the dry clothes.

Hot coffee. The boy poured three mugs of steaming coffee, then reached into a picnic basket for a can of evaporated milk. It was the wicker basket I had seen Bert give Sophie. It hadn't held Jack Parrot at all. It must have held food. I shook my head. Of course, it hadn't held Jack Parrot. Mr. Tate had brought Jack Parrot out in his camera case. I already knew that. I warmed my hands around the hot mug, trying to get my head together.

"Careful, it's hot," I warned Great-Grandpa as he started to take a swallow. His thin hair was plastered down over his forehead like wet strands of yarn. Even his eyebrows drooped.

"I'd forgotten about this playhouse. Father built it when Hugh was a child." I could hardly hear him. It didn't matter. I felt like cheering. He was able to talk. He knew where he was.

"How 'bout us getting some things straight?" the boy said slowly. I guess he still thought we were a couple of idiots. I couldn't blame him. After all, I had sat in a beached boat bailing water like crazy, and I knew my hair must look wild as Brillo. "What was going on down there? What was that man doing?"

The boy had saved us. He deserved an answer. "Mr. Tate was trying to drown us, that's what," I said, getting all upset again at the thought. "He'd found a room full of Chinese treasures in Great-Grandpa's house and wanted it for himself. When Great-Grandpa and I found the room, he figured he'd better get rid of us."

The hot coffee began to spread through my body the way dye in a biology experiment spreads to every vein in a leaf. I was beginning to feel better. "How did you find us?"

"I was on the cove beach checking my boat against the storm when I saw a light come down the path. I hid." The boy's voice was a normal speed. He must have decided we weren't idiots after all. "I saw a big man with some kind of bayonet push you out in the dory, then wade back to shore and take off for the house. He had to be out of his mind. I launched my boat and went after you. That tide was going out, and you were drifting real fast. If it hadn't been for that dog barking, I'd never 'a found you."

Dash. He lay at Great-Grandpa's feet with his tongue out almost to the floor. I bent down and hugged him. His fur smelled sour, like wet wool. It beat any smell in the world.

All of a sudden my spirits lifted. We were safe. And dry.

Even the slap of rain on the pine boughs above us sounded good. Now I could afford to be curious about our rescuer. "What's your name? How did you get here?"

He poured us all more coffee. Then he looked at me for a minute. Wild hair, glasses, braces, peeling nose and all, he must have seen something he trusted. "I'm Ed McBride. Bert Smith's my uncle. I've been living here since April. You saw me down by the dock one of those first days you were here, remember? After that I had to find a new hiding place for my boat and lie real low."

He had succeeded. Mom and I had searched everywhere and never found a trace of him. As for being Bert's nephew, that was reason enough for Bert and Sophie to help him.

But Great-Grandpa wasn't satisfied. "Why are you hiding, boy?"

Ed McBride shrugged his shoulders. "I'll be eighteen August twenty-third. Then I'm my own free man."

What kind of answer was that? Everyone in the world was ripping off Great-Grandpa and didn't even feel they owed him an explanation. Or thanks. "What right do you have to hide here? Are you stealing from Great-Grandpa, too?" I demanded.

"I am not. All I done is hide," Ed retorted. He took another swallow of coffee. It seemed to calm him down. "My mother is Bert's sister. We live over to Portsmouth. My parents got divorced last year, and I went to live with my dad. Ma made a legal fuss to get me back. I wouldn't go. For lots of reasons. Then Ma's lawyer really put the screws on. So I took off for Uncle Bert's. He knew how I felt. He set me up here till I'm eighteen. Then I can live where I want. That's all there is to it."

The anger drained out of me like air from a punctured balloon. I knew how it felt to be pulled two ways by a divorce.

"I'd say it was lucky for you I *was* hiding here." Ed McBride scowled at us defiantly.

I looked over at Great-Grandpa in his funny low chair with Dash stretched out at his feet. Then I looked at Ed. It was true. We all were alive. And safe. What we'd do tomorrow about Mr. Tate and getting off the island didn't matter right now. I felt the corners of my mouth turn up. What started out as a smile became a full-fledged grin. Lucky wasn't exactly the word.

TWENTY-FOUR

The Eavesdropper

Whoop. Whoop. Whoop. The familiar sound was far away. A police car roaring up First Avenue, that's what it was. I tried to roll over in bed, but I couldn't. I was all tangled up in a prickly blanket. Suddenly I was awake. And sitting up. I was on Shag Island in a playhouse, hiding from Mr. Tate. Great-Grandpa was in a sleeping bag next to me, snoring so loud I was surprised he didn't wake himself up. Dash was asleep at his feet, snoring, too. The boy was gone. Ed Something. Ed McBride. Still wrapped in my blanket, I stood up. A little clock on the table said five ten. No wonder it was so dark. I put on my wet sneakers and tiptoed to the door.

The rain had stopped. And so had the wind. It was still enough to hear the water weeping off the pine trees. The bell buoy clanged softly. A gull called down by the water's edge. Another gull answered. It was gray out, but not the gray of bad weather. Just the gray of early morning.

Whoop. Whoop. Whoop. There it was again, clearer now that I was outside. Then I saw the movement of someone coming through the mist toward me. After last night I would have thought nothing could scare me again, but I clutched my blanket around me like a suit of armor. I poised, ready to run in either direction. The figure drew closer. It was Ed McBride.

"So you're up." He looked pretty uptight, too. "That's the Coast Guard siren. Your friend must have called them over the old man's radio."

"The radio doesn't work. Mr. Tate cut the wire." I was pleased at how calm I sounded. Inside I was churning, and had to force myself to think logically. First things first. "We have to reach the Coast Guard so they can get us off Shag Island." That came before anything else.

But Ed put that down fast. "You think I'm gonna turn myself in now that I've stuck it out all this time? Forget it."

Ed glared at me. When I had first seen Ed I thought he looked tough. Now I changed tough to determined. He meant it. And after all, he had done enough for us. I couldn't ask him to do more. "Okay, I'll go myself. Take care of Great-Grandpa until I get back." I handed Ed my blanket.

"Don't count on me hanging around. I'm gonna stay outta sight till everyone's gone." He didn't ask me to keep his secret. I guess he knew he didn't have to.

I figured the playhouse was about in the middle of the

island, halfway between the back cove and the front dock. As I started out, the sky was brightening, but the brush and pine trees were thick. And dripping. My hair and Ed's big sweatshirt were so wet it might as well still have been raining.

Whoop. Whoop. Whoop. The siren was closer now. The boat must be headed for the dock. At least I hoped it was. The trees began to thin out, and the way became rockier underfoot. Then I remembered Ed had taken a path along the cliff edge the day he had picked up his duffel bag from Bert. All I had to do was find the path, and it would lead me to the dock.

I started to make my way down. There were low bushes and a few straggly trees clinging to the rocks, but they weren't sturdy enough to hold on to. And the rocks were slippery. Lucky for me I was wearing my sneakers. I worked on the diagonal, step by step. Then sure enough, I saw it. A narrow ledge that ran parallel to the water and led to the dock. And there was the Coast Guard cutter. The white boat with its blue stripe and the American flag flying from its stern looked so great, so official, I could practically hear "The Star-Spangled Banner" in the background. Two coastguardsmen jumped onto the dock and tied her up.

Then I saw who else was on board. Roger and Bert. And Sophie. At this hour in the morning? "Roger!" I yelled.

But no one heard me. Just as I called out, there was a bellow from the top of the cliff stairs. It was a man's voice outshouting me.

"HEY THERE!"

All heads on the dock swung upward. Mine too. It was Doug Tate at the top of the cliff stairs, waving his arms. I didn't know seeing him would be such a shock. My stomach flipped. I couldn't face him. I wouldn't. In a crouch, I ran along the ledge, counting on the low shrubbery to hide me. There was a cluster of bayberry bushes right beside the path, about twenty feet from the cliff steps. I ducked down behind them, praying Ed's gray sweatshirt and faded jeans would blend into the scenery.

"Did you find them? Are they safe?" I heard Mr. Tate shout.

What in the world was he talking about?

Sophie was puzzled, too. "What do you mean, find them?" There was no voice in the world like Sophie's. Now it had an edge of panic that made it even shriller.

"Lester and Kimball. They're gone. I can't find them." This time Mr. Tate's voice sounded closer, and I heard his heavy footsteps pound down the cliff steps just beyond me. I froze like a frightened rabbit. I just hoped I was as well camouflaged.

"God in heaven!" Sophie shrieked. She clutched her big bosom.

"All right, talk plain," one of the coastguardsmen ordered. "This boy alerted us to a possible situation out here. What's up?"

This boy. He must mean Roger. Roger was on the ball, all right. *He* had called the Coast Guard.

I could see the dock, but not Mr. Tate. His voice carried so clearly I figured he must be standing right at the bottom of the steps. "Lester went completely crazy last night. He was ranting and raving about Chinese ghosts and music and I don't know what else. Kim was so frightened she asked me to spend the night. I got Lester to bed. Then about one o'clock I heard a commotion. When I went to check, I found I'd been locked in my room. Lester must have done it. By the time I got out he and the girl were gone. I've searched everywhere for them. Everywhere! I even circled the island in my Whaler this morning. The old dory is missing. . . . I . . . I found two oars floating in the water." There was a catch in his throat as if he couldn't go on. "But I can't believe they'd go out . . . not at night . . . in that storm. . . ."

What a performance. A real first-class actor. I knew I should show myself. I *wanted* to show myself. But the thought of facing Mr. Tate paralyzed me. I looked down at the dock. Sophie was as white as if every drop of blood had drained from her face. She swayed against Bert, and he put his arm around her. He looked sick himself. Roger's brown eyes were round as chocolate M&M's.

"Hell," swore the coastguardsman. "They wouldn't have had a chance in that storm."

That finished Sophie. She started to cry. Bert took off his cap and ran his fingers through his thin hair over and over. Roger just stood there, chewing away at his gum, his freckles all blotchy in his pale face.

"When I saw that the radio wire was cut, I sh—sh—shoulda reported it right away," Roger stammered.

"Lester cut that wire. I tell you he was like a madman." Mr. Tate pulled himself together long enough to blame that on Great-Grandpa, too.

That finished me. All of a sudden I wanted everyone to know what kind of rat Mr. Tate really was. And to heck with the risk.

"It's me, Kim." The scared rabbit sprang up from her hiding place. "I'm safe. So is Great-Grandpa. And Dash, too." I started to run along the path toward the dock. But I must have jumped up too fast. The blood rushed from my head, and I got as dizzy as when I ride the whip on the boardwalk. And my stomach heaved the same way, too. I shut my eyes and clenched my teeth to get hold of myself.

It must have been only a couple of seconds before I opened my eyes. But not a person had moved. Just like in a game of freeze-tag, all the players had been stopped in time and space. And they were all staring up at me.

TWENTY-FIVE

Bert and Sophie

If there had been anything to laugh about I would have. Everyone's mouth hung open like they were puppets on a string. Mr. Tate may have been acting before, but he sure wasn't now. People in movies always stagger back with bad news, but this was the first time I had seen anyone really do it. Mr. Tate reeled back against the stair railing.

"Mr. Tate put Great-Grandpa and Dash and me out in that rowboat. He tried to drown us." Then I stopped short. The words sounded ridiculous. It hadn't really happened. It couldn't have. But at that moment Mr. Tate turned on his heel and charged back up the cliff steps three at a time.

It snapped them all out of their trances. Mouths shut. Sophie started across the dock toward me. Bert slapped his cap back on his head. The coastguardsman ran to the bottom of the stairs.

"Stop, sir, stop!" he shouted.

Mr. Tate never broke his stride.

"Stop, sir, and explain yourself," the man in charge yelled again. With no results. Mr. Tate had almost reached the top of the stairs.

"Go after him!" the officer ordered, signaling to the other two sailors. They had guns in their holsters. Real guns. Don't shoot. The thought was so strong in my mind I wasn't sure whether I said it aloud or not. It didn't matter. The sailors ran up the cliff stairs after Mr. Tate without touching their guns.

"He has a Whaler on the back cove beach." The idea just popped into my head and out my mouth. But I knew that's where Mr. Tate was headed. He would run around The Anchorage and down to his boat.

"There's a little inlet on the other side of the island," Bert explained. "I can show you where it is."

The coastguardsman was all business. "Take us there," he directed. I didn't know Bert could move so fast. He sprinted across the dock.

With a roar and a belch of black smoke, the cutter started up just as Bert jumped in. I ran the rest of the way to the dock and watched them go. Gulls wheeled overhead as the boat swung out into the bay. The sight of the American flag briskly waving reassured me. Somehow I just knew everything would be all right.

But Sophie was still worried. "Where's Lester?"

How could I have forgotten? "He's in the old playhouse, and he's all right. I think. At least he was asleep when I left him. It was Ed McBride who rescued us and hid us in the playhouse so Mr. Tate couldn't find us."

Sophie looked at me hard. "Ed McBride, huh? Good for Ed. Let's go. I want to see how Lester is for myself."

Sophie knew the way, an easier way than I had taken. And she marched along double-quick time so that Roger and I had to run to keep up with her.

"Man, that's some wild story. What was Doug Tate up to, anyways?" Roger called over his shoulder as I dogtrotted along behind him.

"Wait up, Roger." I had to tell him how glad I was he had trusted me. And done something about it. We slowed to a walk. "You believed me, didn't you? Your bringing out the Coast Guard was great."

"I thought you'd lost it when you told me that crazy story," Roger said. "But when I fixed the dining-room shutter, I saw the radio wire had been cut. As soon as we landed in Watoset, I called Mr. Tate like you asked. Then, when Mr. Tate didn't come back, I was sorta worried. So I got in touch with the Coast Guard. They called Bert, and Bert called Sophie. That's how come we arrived together like a whole battalion."

"Well, I'm glad you did. What if Mr. Tate had found us in that playhouse?" Sword and all. I shivered. I never wanted to see Mr. Tate again.

Just as Ed had promised, he was gone when Sophie, Roger, and I reached the playhouse. We found Great-

Grandpa alone, seated in his low chair drinking coffee with Dash at his feet. There were dark circles under his eyes, and his face was gaunt. But his eyes were bright, and he looked even better than I had hoped.

And he was as sharp as ever. When he saw Sophie, he lowered his mug, and his beetly eyebrows drew into a frown. "I'm surprised to see you back, Sophie. Forging my name. Cashing my checks. Selling Father's stamps. What got into you?"

His attack took Sophie by surprise. She stared at Great-Grandpa a minute, then plopped her big handbag on the floor. No one put Sophie down for long. "You were poking around in my room?"

"Ayuh, and I'm not proud of it. But I knew you were up to something, and I had to find out what."

"What I was up to was your own doing, Lester," Sophie retorted. "You've always been impossible about money. You just figgered it grew on trees. Your hospital bills was sky-high. Tax money was due. Heating costs was outta sight. What money you had coming in wasn't near enough to cover it all. I didn't know what to do. Ever since last spring you been acting like such an odd stick, I was afraid you were losing your mind like your father. I just couldn't bring myself to tell you how bad things was financially."

"Now hold it." Great-Grandpa shook his finger at Sophie. "You don't know what was going on——"

"Now *you* hold it till I'm finished. Then you can have

your say," Sophie interrupted. "I used my own money, even borrowed some. Then last May I took down those landing drapes to wash 'em and came on those letters in that funny hiding place. Bert's always been a stamp collector, so I had some inkling how much those stamps was worth. And I was right. But not a cent of that money did I spend on myself, Lester. I even got receipts for every bit of that stamp money I paid out." Sophie wasn't about to let Great-Grandpa get a word in. She plowed ahead.

"It was to save you the fret and worry I did it. Even so, you kept looking worse and worse. I thought you oughtta get out of The Anchorage, but I knew you'd never sell. What you needed was family. So I wrote Margaret and Kimball in your handwriting asking 'em to come up, hoping that would help. To tell the truth, Bert's been at me to get married for a good spell now, but I wanted to wait till you was settled."

Bert and Sophie married. Of course. Why hadn't I seen it? Their whispering and funny looks hadn't been plotting at all. They were lovers. I nudged Roger with my elbow.

Roger shrugged and just kept clacking away at his gum. He was about as romantic as one of his mountain men.

The frown eased off Great-Grandpa's face. "Married, eh? Well, that is something. But you should have told me. We could have worked it out. There's plenty of room for you and Bert to live in The Anchorage." His voice turned stern. "And you should have told me my money affairs were so bad, too. That wasn't right, Sophie, and what you did about it wasn't right either. And you know it. Leastways, there's no money problem now. Once I pay duty and taxes and whatever's owed on Father's curios, I'd wager some of those things will bring a handsome price."

"What do you mean, your father's curios?" Sophie asked.

But Great-Grandpa didn't answer her right away. He leaned down and rubbed Dash under the chin. His blue eyes were thoughtful. "The trouble is, Sophie, we didn't trust each other. Father didn't trust anyone with his secret. I didn't trust you with my fears of losing my mind. You didn't trust me with the money matters. That left Douglas Tate ready to profit from the whole thing. And he would have, if Kimball hadn't been around." Great-Grandpa reached out and took my hand.

"I guess that's what roots are for, Great-Grandpa."

In reply, he squeezed my hand. Then he smiled, really smiled at me for the first time since the two of us had been on our own. Dumb tears sprang to my eyes. Great-Grandpa's smiling face blurred as I squeezed his hand in return.

We didn't find out what happened to Doug Tate until Bert came out in the *Lucky Sue* later in the morning to pick up Roger. Bert and the Coast Guard had chased Mr. Tate in his Whaler, catching up to him just as he reached Brink Island down the bay a way. Great-Grandpa would have papers to sign and all sorts of legal stuff to straighten out. But Mr. Tate was caught. And we were safe. Now all that was left to do was wait for Mom to come back.

Great-Grandpa, Sophie, and I spent the rest of the day on the Bridge with Dash asleep in total exhaustion outside the door. With Sophie's help, I had finally caught Jack Parrot. He swung in his cage while I tried to bribe him with peaches into talking. With no success. Great-Grandpa, Sophie, and I had hashed and rehashed everything that had happened. We had even taken a tour of the Curiosity Room. Now we were all talked out.

I had just fed Jack his last piece of peach when I heard the *Lucky Sue*'s bell. Before it had even run twice, I was on my feet. I raced out of the Bridge, through the house, across the yard, and to the top of the cliff stairs. The air was clear enough to see forever. The late-afternoon sun shot sparkles off the water bright as rhinestones. It was as if the storm had blown away the old sky and water and laid down new. And there was Mom climbing out of the *Lucky Sue*. She had on the same yellow and blue dress she had worn when she left, just as if she had never been gone. She was smoking. I was so glad to see her, I didn't care if she had a cigarette in either hand.

"Mom!" She looked up and waved. Waved! As if she expected me to be the same as when she left two and a half days ago. I started down the steps at a run. She put out her arms, and I flew into them like I haven't done since I was three and lost for an hour in Bloomingdale's.

"Easy, Kim," she laughed. "I've had a rough couple of days. I'm so beat you could knock me over with a feather."

Over Mom's shoulder I saw Bert lift her carry-on onto

the dock. I didn't see Roger. He must not have come out this trip. I caught Bert's eye and smiled. He *almost* smiled in return. Mom didn't notice.

"Honestly, I can hardly wait for a quick swim and a hot bath." She lit a fresh cigarette from the stub of her first. "I've put in two days like you wouldn't believe, and the sooner I can forget it, the better. New York was steaming. Mrs. La Bronquist was as impossible as ever. Harvey was on the rampage. All I could think of was Shag Island and this lovely peace and quiet. I thanked heaven you were here soaking it all up and not back with me in that rat race."

"Yeah, Mom, you're right. It's been really peaceful." I tried to keep a straight face, but I started to laugh. It was more than even Bert could stand. He laughed, too.

"Let me in on the joke," Mom said.

"When we get to the house, I promise I'll tell you the whole story," I said. "Let's go. Great-Grandpa's waiting to see you. And Sophie made brownies and iced tea."

"That sounds marvelous." Mom headed for the cliff stairs.

"Sophie wants you to come too, Bert. Can you?" I asked.

"I reckon so. I'm through for the day. But I got some groceries to deliver first." Bert gestured with his thumb over his shoulder.

I looked at where he was pointing. Was that a blond head of hair and a scowling face beyond the pine trees? I wasn't sure, but just in case, I gave a quick wave. Then I picked up Mom's carry-on and followed her up the cliff steps to The Anchorage.